1·50

Knick-Knack

TROLL
IN TRICKLETOWN

Written and Illustrated by
Martin P. Buckley

Supporters of Anti-Bullying

See Dudley's Message about Secrets and Bullying
on page 202

Wiggly-Fish Books
www.wiggly-fish.com

First Published in Great Britain by Wiggly-Fish Books 2015
www.wiggly-fish.com

Author and Illustrator
Martin P. Buckley
The moral right of the author/illustrator has been asserted for this work.

ISBN: 978-0-9551918-1-7

Printed in Great Britain by
York Publishing Services Ltd.

British Library Cataloguing in Publication Data
A CIP catalogue record for this book is available from the British Library.
Issue 1 First published October 2015

DEDICATION

This book is dedicated to my family

Paul, Doreen, Hazel & Rachel, Carol & Andrew

and also
to the memory and inspiration of
Ursula Moray Williams
a dear friend
and author of many children's books
including my favourites

The Little Wooden Horse
Gobbolino the Witch's Cat
and
The Little Christmas Tree

A biography of her life *Through The Magic Door*
by Colin Davison

(ISBN: 9780857160065)

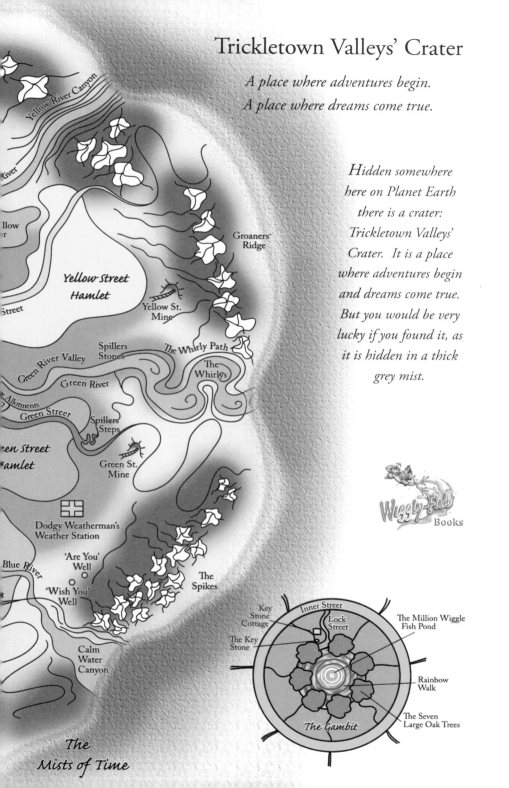

Trickletown Valleys' Crater

A place where adventures begin.
A place where dreams come true.

Hidden somewhere here on Planet Earth there is a crater: Trickletown Valleys' Crater. It is a place where adventures begin and dreams come true. But you would be very lucky if you found it, as it is hidden in a thick grey mist.

Yellow River Canyon

llow r

River

Groaners' Ridge

Yellow Street Hamlet

Street

Yellow St. Mine

Spillers Stones

The Whirly Path

Green River Valley

The Whirlys

Green River

Allotments

Green Street

Spillers Steps

en Street amlet

Green St. Mine

Dodgy Weatherman's Weather Station

'Are You' Well

The Spikes

Blue River

'Wish You' Well

Calm Water Canyon

Wiggly-Fish Books

Key Stone Cottage

Inner Street

Lock Street

The Million Wiggle Fish Pond

The Key Stone

Rainbow Walk

The Gambit

The Seven Large Oak Trees

The Mists of Time

Trickletown Valleys' Crater

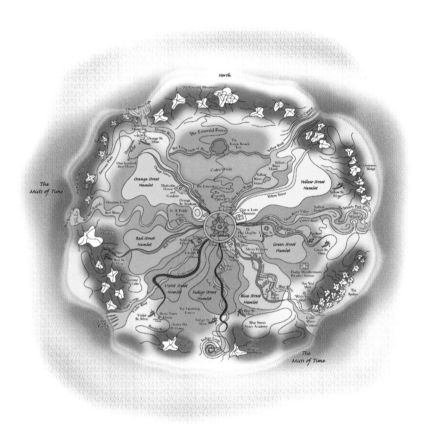

A place where adventures begin.
A place where dreams come true.

TROUBLE IN TRICKLETOWN

- Chapter 1 -

The Fuddles Build Tricketown

Hidden somewhere here on Planet Earth there is a crater: Tricketown Valleys' Crater. It is a place where adventures begin and dreams come true. But you would be very lucky if you found it, as it is hidden in a thick grey mist.

Many millions of years ago, and long before life on Planet Earth had even had the chance to exist, the Crater was not very important at all, just a dusty shallow crater. Nothing grew here, nothing lived here, and certainly nothing ever came here. Until one day, out of the stillness of space and from somewhere beyond the Moon, something magical happened!

Its arrival was nothing out of the ordinary, as by all accounts it was just another shooting star – a small insignificant object twinkling in the sky very briefly, before tumbling to the ground, never to be thought of again.

But this particular shooting star had not just arrived here – it had been sent! This small, orange object, only the size and shape of a coconut had tumbled onto the slopes of the Crater.

A small cloud of dust was all that marked the object's arrival, but before the dust had settled, magical things began to happen.

A tiny white root wriggled free and began tunnelling itself into the ground. It was followed very closely by another and soon by several more.

The clouds above the Crater blackened and lightning crackled in the skies. The roots grew larger … Soon they became so big that the ground beneath the Crater started to move.

The roots formed living labyrinths beneath the surface and pushed snow capped mountains high around the Crater's edge. Soon seven rivers flowed down seven valleys and on the northern slope of the Crater, where the shooting star had landed, a curious living tree had started to grow.

To begin with it looked like any other tree, but this tree was different! Very different! This tree was not just living, it could breathe – it was alive! Soon a face appeared, and two eyes opened. As its large mouth yawned; its breath swept a carpet of life across the Crater's floor. The Knick-Knack Tree had arrived and the Crater had changed for ever.

So what was this all about? What was the Knick-Knack Tree … and why was it here?

Well what happened next begins to answer these questions.

A large number of Fuddles arrived in the Crater.

Fuddles were human like us, but they had evolved to be slightly different. In addition to some other curious things *(which the Knick-Knack Tree Adventures will reveal)*, they appeared to have ears a little larger or smaller than what you might call normal and they were also super-intelligent and never forget a single thing they were told.

They had travelled to this Crater from their homes on a small orange planet called Fuddle, hiding secretly behind Earth's Moon. If you look very carefully you can sometimes see it, especially when the Moon is full and the glow around the edge of it is orange.

On arrival, they emerged from beyond a Sizing Stone, one of a series of magical stones which protect the very small entrances to the Knick-Knack Tree's passageways, treasures and secrets. These stones would alter their size (small to go in and back to full size when coming out again), this allowed the Fuddles to move in and out of these entrances with ease. However, these stones would only allow anyone to enter if their intentions were good!

The Fuddles emerged from beyond a Sizing Stone, one of a series of magical stones which protect the very small entrances to the Knick-Knack Tree's passageways, treasures and secrets. These stones would alter their size (small to go in and back to full size when coming out again).

This particular Sizing Stone sat outside the entrance to the hole at the base of the Knick-Knack Tree's trunk. The hole was the entrance to a den, from where doors and passageways led to places deep inside the Tree's roots and – provided you could find your way around them – they could take you anywhere you wished.

The Fuddles had arrived in Trickletown Valleys' Crater for a reason. They needed a safe place to keep their fish! The Million Wiggle Fish were colourful intelligent fish with powers of their own – powers so extraordinary that everyone in the Universe wanted them. When the Fuddles first found these mysterious fish, in deep, dark caverns beneath the surface of Planet Fuddle, everything had started off well. Space travellers came from far and wide to buy the magnificent fish and have fun with them. The fish could help them travel through time; they could take them to places we could only dream about; and they could warn them and guide them away from danger … In fact one or another of these colourful fish could do almost anything you imagined. Each type was a different colour of the rainbow.

But Trouble was brewing – the mysterious Mists of Time (the Fuddles' arch enemy) wanted these fish for themselves and were prepared to do anything to get hold of them! The Mists of Time were dangerous. They had a mind of their own. The mist inside them was so thick, that the past, the present, and the future tangled together. You could soon get lost, and there are many Fuddles who have entered them who have never been seen again.

The surface of the newly formed Crater changed again, as the Fuddles built Trickletown. Seven hamlets full of colourful houses soon appeared between the seven river valleys; and seven cobbled streets, each one paved in a different colour of the rainbow, wound past forests and mountains.

*The Million Wiggle Fish were colourful intelligent fish with powers of their own
– powers so extraordinary that everyone in the Universe wanted them.*

Inside a circular road named Inner Street, the Fuddles left an area of grass they called 'The Gambit'.

It was a place where they could go to think, but The Gambit was so much more than just an area of grass. Mysterious and magical things could happen here and in the Knick-Knack Tree Adventures they often do!

The Gambit

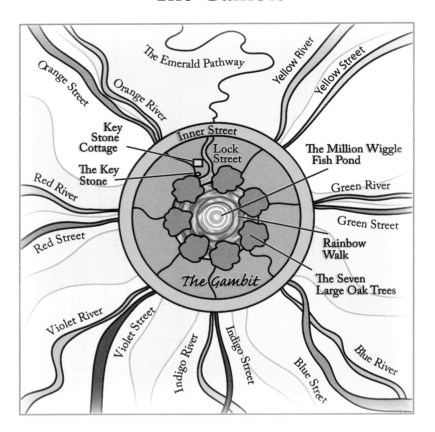

At the centre of The Gambit, inside a ring of seven large oak trees, the Fuddles built a fish pond – 'The Million Wiggle Fish Pond' – and this was the brand new home for their precious fish. The fountain of the pool was made from living granite and this brand new wonder of the universe could change its shape to whatever it liked.

The pool was guarded by seven Rainbow Fish. These seven living, stone fish hovered around the edge of the pool in globes of water. Each one was a different colour of the rainbow, and large enough to sit on, which was something they occasionally let you do.

Floating above the centre of the fountain, looking out over the tops of the seven oak trees, hovered one very clever, living, stone fish. This one was silver and gold and its job was to look out for trouble!

Surrounding the fish pond, there was something even more magical! A spiral passageway through time, called Rainbow Walk. This was truly a magical place – 'a place where adventures begin and dreams come true'.

The Million Wiggle Fish Pond – surrounded by Rainbow Walk.

The magical Million Wiggle Fish Pond, besides being a home for the Million Wiggle Fish, was built to protect them. In times of danger a brightly coloured mosaic barrier sealed the surface. Then, when the Hour Glass Key was placed in the Granite Key Stone, the fish pond lowered itself beneath the ground and was hidden away from its enemies by the surface of The Gambit. Its position could then be locked by placing the stone from the Emerald Ring in its slot, at the centre of the Hour Glass Key.

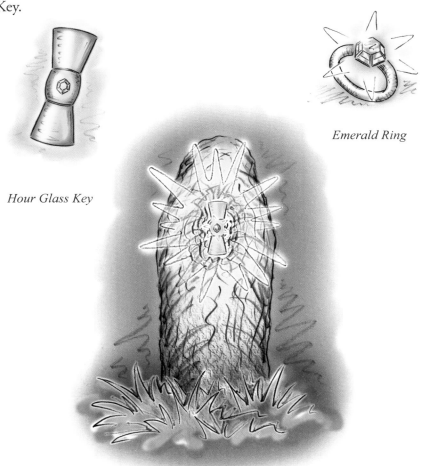

Emerald Ring

Hour Glass Key

The Hour Glass Key and the Stone of the Emerald Ring, locked in their place at the centre of the Granite Key Stone.

Life in Trickletown Valleys' Crater became great fun. The Knick-Knack Tree and the inhabitants of Trickletown appeared to be safe in their brand new homes, and travellers began to arrive from every corner of the universe to purchase the Million Wiggle Fish.

These travellers began telling of their adventures, and as each new story was told, a brand new Knick-Knack was hung on the Knick-Knack Tree's branches. It reminded everyone of the story. Soon the Tree was covered from root to twig in a glorious collection of Knick-Knacks.

A tiny elf-like character called Knicky-Knacky began telling the stories of these adventures. He lived in a cosy den among the Tree's roots, and whenever a Knick-Knack was chosen, he would appear from his den and begin to tell everyone its story …

The first of these stories to be told was **Trouble in Trickletown**.

- Chapter 2 -

The Story Begins

Excitement was beginning to build in the Emerald Forest. The Knick-Knack Tree was awake and an adventure was about to be chosen.

'That one!' shouted a mouse, pointing to a shiny gold Knick-Knack, hanging high in the Knick-Knack Tree's branches. It was a gold medallion and on it had been etched the words:

'A place where adventures begin.
A place where dreams come true'.

Knicky-Knacky retrieved it from the branches and then, sitting on his favourite log, he began to tell everyone its story ...

"The Mists of Time had surrounded Trickletown Valleys' Crater. Their plan was to steal the Million Wiggle Fish and take over Trickletown.

"The Hour Glass Key had been stolen.

"The Emerald Ring was now missing.

Emerald Ring

Hour Glass Key

"And the seven Rainbow Fish who guarded the magical Million Wiggle Fish Pond were nowhere to be found!

The Seven Rainbow Fish — each one a different colour of the Rainbow.

"And this was only the start of it. The What'Nott family and Mr Got-a-Lott were all in desperate trouble."

Knicky-Knacky fidgeted around on his log, just to make sure he was perfectly comfortable.

"The What'Nott family live in Key Stone Cottage, right next door to the Million Wiggle Fish Pond at the centre of the Gambit.

Mr What'Nott was tall, dark and handsome, and as wearer of the Emerald Ring he was the most important Fuddle in Trickletown.

Mrs What'Nott   *Mr What'Nott*

"Mrs What'Nott was fine-looking too, and just as important, for she looked after their children, Willey and Casey, and their pet dog Badsey – a loving, but lively Jack Russell Terrier.

Casey, Badsey and Willey

"Willey What'Nott was our Knick-Knack Tree Adventurer.

He was fascinated by the Moon and the Stars, and spent many hours looking out over the dark night sky from his bedroom window. He was very easy to recognise, with a glorious well-kept crest of ginger hair, and usually dressed in a T-shirt and jeans, plus a bright red jacket. Casual but smart, as he liked to call it; and always ready for an adventure.

"Casey was just like her mother. Although she was younger than Willey, she secretly did her best to follow him on many of his adventures.

Willey What'Nott

"The Last of our Fuddles in Trouble was Mr Got-a-Lott. He was large and round and always dressed in different shades of yellow. He was the owner of the Got-a-Lott Museum – a place which kept something of everything; almost everything you can think of from the past and many things not even invented yet, from some time in the future."

Mr Got-a-Lott

19

As the story continued, and the crowd around the Knick-Knack Tree grew larger, the magical pollen from its blossoms floated down onto them. Soon, the adventure appeared real!

It was as if they were all becoming part of it.

*

The trouble in Trickletown began when a troublesome comet called Climaticus was circling the Earth. It was stirring up winds around Trickletown; and the dangerous Mists of Time were moving nearer to the centre of the Crater. This was their chance to steal the fish and they were determined to take it.

Mr What'Nott was going to need help to secure the fish pond safely beneath the surface of The Gambit.

Mrs What'Nott, Willey and Mr Got-a-Lott arrived to help – but to keep themselves safe outside in the Mists of Time, they each made

themselves an extra body; now there were two identical versions of each of them. This was what most fuddles do in times of danger. These extra bodies of Mr and Mrs What'Nott, Willey and Mr Got-a-Lott returned to Key Stone Cottage, where they remained with Willey's sister Casey and the pet dog Badsey. Here they hoped to stay safe as the Mists of Time swirled around the Crater. But things went wrong.

The Mists of Time forced their way in through a narrow gap beneath the cottage front door. The extra body of Mr Got-a-Lott was dragged outside, where The Mists of Time forced him to steal the Hour Glass Key and the Rainbow Fish and run away with them. They tried to make him seize the Emerald Ring from Mr What'Nott's fingers … but it fell to the ground. As the surface of The Gambit closed and the fish pond disappeared, a mysterious hand reached out and grabbed the Emerald Ring!

The Mists of Time now covered everything …

The Million Wiggle Fish Pond was now trapped beneith the surface of the Gambit.

Key Stone Cottage and everyone inside it spiralled away in the mist to sometime in the future. The other versions of Mr and Mrs What'Nott and Mr Got-a-Lott had also been affected by The Mists of Time, but they all remained in Trickletown Valleys' Crater. Now they are helping the Mists of Time take over Trickletown. The other Willey What'Nott had managed to escape, but it might only be a matter of time before they captured him.

- Chapter 3 -

A Mysterious Orange Envelope

To follow our Knick-Knack Tree Adventure we must travel through time, to find the What'Nott family who had remained in Key Stone Cottage when the trouble began.

They had thought they would all remain safe when the other versions of Mr and Mrs What'Nott, Willey and Mr Got-a-Lott ventured out into the Mists of Time to lock the Million Wiggle Fish Pond safely beneath the surface of the Gambit. But the Mists of Time captured the cottage and moved everyone hiding inside it to some time in the future. They are still inside Key Stone Cottage, at the centre of The Gambit, but everything around them has changed. It appeared to have all been hidden inside a circle of thick grey mist.

Inside Key Stone Cottage everything for the moment was quiet. Most of the What'Nott family had gone to bed, except that is for Willey; as he couldn't sleep. It might just have been the fact that tomorrow was his birthday. He would be nine years old and – to add to the suspense – his special birthday surprise had not yet been revealed. But there were other things worrying him too: how could he possibly return back to the correct time? The Trickletown Valleys' Games were due to begin in only two days time and he was desperate to win the Chaseboard Challenge Race for Orange Street. He missed his best friend Eddy, who lived in Trickletown, and he longed to see the Knick-Knack Tree again and listen to Knicky-Knacky tell of its stories and adventures. But nothing he could think of appeared possible – Key Stone Cottage and everyone inside it were lost in time and for the moment there was no way back again!

Key Stone Cottage, Lock Street, Trickletown –
a cottage all on its own at the centre of Trickletown Valleys' Crater.

The Moon was big and bright and shining in through the bedroom window – in fact there was far too much light for anyone who wanted to sleep.

'A full Moon at last,' thought Willey, looking closer at the lines and shapes he could see over its surface. His attention drifted towards the Moon's edge; not to any particular shape but to a faint orange glow, which he had never noticed before.

This faint orange glow appeared to pulse very slowly – as if it were trying to hold Willey's attention.

It was then that he noticed something else. Two very distinctive eyes were peering back at him, from behind the Moon!

Startled, Willey jumped back and closed the curtains.

It was several worrying moments before his courage returned and he could open them again, but when he did, the two mysterious eyes were nowhere to be seen.

Willey looked at the Moon again and again, but nothing changed. Whatever it was had disappeared. Willey could not stay awake a moment longer and reluctantly returning to his bed, was soon fast asleep.

The Moon was big and bright but Willey had noticed something else;
two very distinctive eyes were peering back at him.

But this was not the end of the matter!

Willey began to dream …

In his dream he was standing on The Gambit, inside the circle of oak trees. He knew exactly where he was, as he could see his rope swing swaying in the background. Seated beside a neatly laid out table was a beautiful and enchanting lady, dressed in a blue satin gown with a Crown of Gold on her head. Willey recognised her: she was the Queen of Fuddles.

Staring back at Willey from the depths of seven jars swam seven colourful, wiggly fish, each one a different colour of the rainbow.

Willey stared at the fish and wondered … and they stared back! 'Million Wiggle Fish,' thought Willey; he was really excited to see some. The picture in Willey's dream began to change – the mysterious Mists of Time rolled in from the mountains and the Knick-Knack Tree's face appeared. It was surrounded by thorns.

A sad, despairing voice began to speak to him:

"Willey we need your help … You must look in a secret place for a Shaft of Sunlight, it will lead you back to Trickletown; to the place where adventures begin and dreams come true, but when you find it you must not be followed … "

The voice had become hesitant and full of emotion.

Nothing more was said. Willey knew something was wrong. Before he could find out more, this dream, like many others before it, came to a sudden end.

The door to Willey's bedroom burst open, "HAPPY BIRTHDAY WILLEY! HAPPY BIRTHDAY!"

Staring back at Willey from the depths of seven jars swam seven colourful,
wiggly fish, each one a different colour of the rainbow.

The words echoed around the room as if Willey's head was stuck inside a biscuit tin, but it was just his sister Casey, his mum and dad and leading the charge, raced Badsey, a very excited Jack Russell Terrier. In no time at all, Badsey had pinned Willey to his pillow and was smothering him in many licks and kisses.

Willey had overslept, and Casey was excitedly trying to find out more about Willey's special birthday surprise.

The answer, she thought, must be in one of the many envelopes now scattered over Willey's bed. She was sure she knew exactly which one it would be in, and was soon offering Willey a bright orange envelope.

"Come on then, open it!" she instructed.

All this attention was becoming a little too much for Willey, who was still not fully awake.

"Calm down, Casey," interrupted Mum, realising the situation was getting a little out of hand. "There will be plenty of time to open all the cards and all the presents, Willey's special birthday surprise is not until later this afternoon – so there is no point searching for clues in all those envelopes!"

Despite this reassurance, Willey was now sitting up in bed and intent on opening the mysterious orange envelope.

"SIT and STAY!" grumbled Mr What'Nott, making sure that Badsey sat on the mat beside Willey's bed, and did as he was told, or else!

Willey was in such a hurry that he didn't even notice the envelope opened itself and placed its contents gently in the palm of his hand – in fact it was only Badsey who noticed anything at all, and gave a cautious growl as the envelope hid under Willey's bed.

Suddenly, the room was filled with Willey's joyful shrieks.

"THE CIRCUS!" he announced, at the top of his voice, "YIPPEE! WE ARE GOING TO THE CIRCUS!"

Suddenly, the room was filled with Willey's joyful shrieks. "THE CIRCUS !"
he announced, at the top of his voice,
"YIPPEE! WE ARE GOING TO THE CIRCUS!"

With one excited leap, Willey shot out of bed and with his sister, marched across the bedroom and down the wooden staircase into the kitchen.

♫ "We're going to the circus, ♫ we're going to the circus!"

They sang the same repetitive tune until they reached the breakfast table, leaving all the other envelopes strewn over Willey's bed and across the bedroom floor. One even found its way into Badsey's mouth, which did not impress Mr What'Nott one bit.

Mr and Mrs What'Nott looked at one another in astonishment. Who on earth had sent Willey a ticket to a circus?

Catching up with the children, Mrs What'Nott held up the mysterious ticket.

It said:

Trickletown Valleys' Circus is proud to invite
Willey What'Nott and his family
to a Special Circus Performance.
The Circus will begin this afternoon
and take place on Trickletown Gambit.

Finally, beneath a glittering picture of a magnificent circus tent were the words:

Please be ready at 2 o'clock.

Willey What'Nott's Ticket to the Trickletown Valleys' Circus,
delivered by the mysterious Orange Envelope.

For the rest of Willey's birthday, until 2 o'clock at least, it was just like any other birthday, with lots of fun and laughter, chocolate cake, presents and sweets.

- Chapter 4 -

Trickletown Valleys' Circus

As the clock struck two, there was a rhythmic 'Rat-a-Tat-Tat' on the front door.

The What'Notts, all over-excited, dashed towards it, but had only got half-way down the hall when the door flew open.

In stepped a very smart gentleman, dressed in a fine black moleskin suit, trimmed with gold.

He removed his splendid matching hat and, without speaking a single word, he beckoned them through the door and down the garden path to the front gate of the cottage.

There the What'Notts stood in utter astonishment, as standing right in front of them, within the circle of oak trees, stood a magnificent circus tent, the very circus tent that had been pictured on the mysterious ticket!

No one even bothered to question how it had managed to appear outside their front gate. They were far too excited to think about anything quite so trivial. The gate swung open too, and before you could say the words 'Knick-Knack Tree Adventures', the smartly dressed gentleman ushered his guests the final few metres towards the entrance to the mysterious Trickletown Valleys' Circus.

As the clock struck two, there was a rhythmic 'Rat-a-Tat-Tat' on the front door. In stepped a very smart gentleman dressed in a fine black moleskin suit, trimmed with gold.

"Welcome," said the Ticket Collector, in a deep, distinctive voice. "Welcome to the greatest show on Earth."

'Wow!' thought Willey, taking a deep breath and believing every word the large, round Ticket Collector was telling him. 'The greatest show on Earth!'

Casey grabbed hold of Willey's hand as they slowly inched their way around the Ticket Collector's large, round body. Willey wasn't entirely certain that he couldn't see straight through him – and they both noticed he was wearing a false moustache.

Despite the false moustache and his faint appearance, Willey knew exactly who this was. It was his mum and dad's friend, Mr Got-a-Lott. The owner of the Got-a-Lott Museum and now it appeared, quite strangely, that he was a part of the Trickletown Valleys' Circus!

PSSSST! The large, round Ticket Collector sprayed the air around them, with what looked like a can of air freshener. "Helps to keep the insects away," he said, winking his eye at Willey. "Plenty of those around the circus."

These actions appeared rather suspicious!

Mr What'Nott paused to think about things, "Umm … What you need to remember about the circus," he said, "is that not everything is as it might seem." It appeared that Mr What'Nott had also spotted the false moustache! "And don't go running off, you might get lost."

With the large, round Ticket Collector behind them, the What'Notts continued on their journey to the circus tent. Their progress was only briefly interrupted by a hairy orangutan, handing out the circus programmes.

"Well I never," said Mr What'Nott, as he politely took a programme for himself.

Willey and Casey could only smile as a tiny marmoset, perched on his shoulders, grinned right back at them.

"Welcome," said the Ticket Collector, in a deep, distinctive voice.
"Welcome to the greatest show on Earth."

"WOW!" said each of the What'Notts as they entered the circus tent. It was truly a magnificent sight.

"Over there!" shouted Mr What'Nott, breaking the moment of silence and pointing towards a row of spare seats beside the musicians' stand. There was certainly no time to waste, as the circus was filling up fast.

With only a little bit of barging and the occasional polite apology, the What'Notts manoeuvred their way towards the musicians' stand and breathed a sigh of relief as they settled into their seats.

Willey looked up in awe at the magnificent circus tent. It was big and bright and round, and it reminded him of the Moon he had been watching from his bedroom window. It was then that something familiar caught his eye!

Above the circus ring, in bright gold letters were the words: *'A place where adventures begin. A place where dreams come true'*.

Willey began to think. Where had he heard these words before?

It was then he remembered his dream!

He remembered the Queen of Fuddles and her jars of Million Wiggle Fish. He remembered the Knick-Knack Tree's face surrounded by thorns and the mist rolling in from the mountains ...

The voice from Willey's dream began to speak to him again: "You must look in a secret place for a Shaft of Sunlight, which will lead you back to Trickletown, but when you find it you must not be followed."

Willey was now certain that the circus was his way back to Trickletown. Now all he had to do was wait until whoever it was who brought him here showed him the way to the rest of his adventure.

With only a little bit of barging and the occasional polite apology, the What'Notts manoeuvred their way towards the musicians' stand and breathed a sigh of relief as they settled into their seats.

- Chapter 5 -

A Billion Specks of Gold Dust

The circus tent was full and bristling with excitement.

'There must be some clues around here somewhere,' thought Willey; especially if the circus tent was hiding his way back to Trickletown. To Willey's left, on a raised wooden platform, rested a number of musical instruments, each one brightly decorated with a colourful selection of flowers and Million Wiggle Fish. 'More of those wiggly fish,' thought Willey; they appeared to be popping up everywhere.

The circus ring in front of him was covered in a thick layer of sawdust and surrounded by a curved box wall. Several people were sitting on it, content to just gaze about at the audience as they took up the last remaining seats.

Willey noticed not everyone was sitting down: many just wandered about not chatting to anyone in particular and then they wandered out again. It was almost as if the circus was a meeting place – but there must be more to it than this?

In time, the circus ring emptied and the noise began to fade to an expectant hush. A drum roll set the scene from behind the curtains. Then suddenly, bursting in from the shadows and accompanied by an enormous fire cracker, appeared the awe-inspiring figure of the Ring Master, superbly dressed in a shimmering black moleskin suit, trimmed with gold.

"Welcome!" said the Ring Master. "Welcome to the Trickletown Valleys' Circus!"

This spectacular entrance was greeted by a deafening cheer.

Then suddenly, bursting in from the shadows and accompanied by an enormous fire cracker, appeared the awe-inspiring figure of the Ring Master.

"Today, ladies and gentlemen, boys and girls, you will witness unbelievable feats of trickery and balance.

"You will be amazed by astounding acts of mystery and magic.

"But first, opening our show this afternoon, please welcome from Indigo Street, here in Trickletown, the only act ever to attempt the terrifying hoops of fire, the high wire act that is: "The Balancing Cubonyento Brothers!"

W O O O S S H!

A flash of fire lit up the circus ring and through a giant hoop of flames dived the three Cubonyento Brothers, tumbling into the centre of the circus ring.

Before Willey could gather his thoughts, the Cubonyentos had climbed up to a long thin wire and began to amaze the audience with mesmerising tricks and tumbles and death defying leaps and twists. The audience gasped and gripped their seats and the What'Notts watched in utter astonishment.

The circus continued with Willey and his family enjoying every minute of it. But the circus was not the only reason everyone was there. There was something else.

Something very mysterious was happening, and Willey was soon to find out what it was!

A flash of fire lit up the circus ring and through a giant hoop of flames dived the three Cubonyento Brothers, tumbling into the centre of the circus ring.

Willey's mind was wandering. His thoughts were moving away from the sounds of the circus – he was hearing different sounds. Soft and fairly distant ones at first but gradually becoming clearer. So clear in fact that when Willey closed his eyes, he began to believe he was actually somewhere else. But he couldn't be, could he? Willey checked and double-checked by opening and closing his eyes. Everything around him stayed the same – it was just the sounds that were different.

Willey closed his eyes again – and kept them shut. He was sure he could hear the calls of animals on the other side of the tent: moos and bleats, grunts and the distant sounds of chatting and shouting. This all sounded more like a busy market place than a circus!

Then Willey noticed something else!

A narrow gap had mysteriously appeared beneath the musicians' stand. Through it Willey could see a thin shaft of sunlight – there was an opening at the bottom of the circus tent!

'This is the secret place,' thought Willey. 'The one the voice in my dream spoke about.'

Without a second's thought to the dangers which might lie ahead, Willey took one final glance at his mum and dad and Casey and slipped silently beneath the musicians' stand.

Instantly a flash of lightning lit up the tent and a roll of thunder shook the skies. A dangerous storm was gathering: the Mists of Time were here and trying to stop Willey moving under the tent! His journey to the other side would not be easy.

The circus acts continued to perform, as if nothing out of the ordinary was happening.

The large round Ticket Collector fidgeted. He'd had plenty to do with what was happening, but even he could do no more about it.

A narrow gap had mysteriously appeared beneath the musicians' stand. Through it Willey could see a thin shaft of sunlight – there was an opening at the bottom of the circus tent!

It was time for someone else to take control and she was here – the Queen of Fuddles, the lady in the blue silken gown that Willey had seen in his dream, with the jars of Million Wiggle Fish! She had been waiting for just this moment. Stepping out of the shadows with her arms stretched out before her, she held her Crown of Gold.

"Travel safely," she whispered "but follow only *my* will." With this her Crown of Gold spun from her fingertips and hovered high in the roof of the tent.

The crown began to pulse to the rhythm of her heartbeat as it guarded Willey's safe return to Trickletown.

Willey was almost there. All he needed to do was raise his hand to guide himself to the other side. The crowds in the circus tent fell still as time moved around them. Then suddenly the skies erupted and seven shafts of lightning tore through the tent. The crown began to melt. As drips of molten gold dropped down into the circus ring, flames raced across to the crimson curtains. But it was not the curtains the flames were after – they wanted to put an end to Willey's adventure before it began, by destroying the words in his dream, written high above the circus ring:

A place where adventures begin.
A place where dreams come true.

There was no time to lose! At the lady's final command, the Crown of Gold burst out into a billion specks of gold dust. The flames could move no further and as the gold dust fluttered to the ground, the magnificent circus tent disappeared.

Then suddenly the skies erupted and seven shafts of lightning tore through the tent.

The scene was changing fast. Gone were the thrills of the circus and instead Willey stood in a busy market place, full of the sounds he had been hearing from inside the circus tent.

To begin with it was difficult to move, as Willey pushed his way through the crowd. He knew he was searching for someone and suddenly he found who it was – *another Willey What'Nott appeared in front of him!*

The two of them looked at each other. They both looked exactly the same. They had the same glorious crest of ginger hair and they were dressed in exactly the same clothes: a T-shirt and jeans and a bright red jacket – casual but smart and ready for an adventure.

Following a considerable pause, the two boys raised their hands to touch each other and as soon as their fingertips touched, the two Willey What'Notts became one. It was as if they had both disappeared one inside the other; their two separate worlds became one again.

Willey's journey beneath the circus tent had taken him back through time, and now he was back at the time when the Trouble in Trickletown began.

His enemies knew he was here. But now Willey's two separate minds were back together, he remembered more about the Trouble in Trickletown than anyone else. All the Fuddles were losing their memories, due to a mysterious 'memory-loss' spray Willey's other mum and dad *(the now villainous Mr and Mrs What'Nott, the ones who had remained back in Trickletown)* had been selling in their corner shop. This was the very same spray Mr Got-a-Lott, the large round Ticket Collector, had attempted to spray over the What'Nott's as they entered the Trickletown Valleys' Circus – remember he cunningly told them that it helped to keep the insects away!

All of this extra memory will give Willey an advantage, but only if he is able to avoid any contact with these dangerous sprays. The only problem is, that at this moment, he knows nothing about them. It will be up to the Queen of Fuddles – the lady who brought him here – to warn him about them and quickly.

All the dangers lurking around him had for now disappeared; today was still his birthday, and there were plenty of birthday things still waiting to be done.

*Willey pushed his way through the crowd. He knew he was searching for someone
and suddenly he found who it was – another Willey What'Nott
appeared in front of him!*

- Chapter 6 -

Return of the Orange Envelope

Willey was back in Trickletown. His journey beneath the circus tent had taken him back in time to when the Trouble in Trickletown began. His two separate bodies were back together again and now the mysterious powers which had brought him here could put their plan into action: to send Willey off on an adventure, to help save Trickletown Valleys' Crater from the Mists of Time.

Willey awoke to find things had changed.

His sister, Casey, was missing: she was lost in the Mists of Time with Willey's kind mum and dad and their pet dog Badsey.

Willey's bad mum and dad appeared stricter than before – they were helping the Mists of Time take over Trickletown, so Willey would need to be careful.

Key Stone Cottage and the oak trees were no longer surrounded by mist. Instead, beyond the circle that was Inner Street and divided by seven magnificent river Valleys, lay the seven colourful hamlets of Trickletown. Each one was brightly decorated in a different colour of the rainbow.

"Willey, your breakfast is on the table."

The tone of Mrs What'Nott's voice was not to be ignored so Willey ate his breakfast without fuss. Anyway he couldn't wait to get started looking for clues to his adventure.

Once outside, Willey shouted "Manual One," jumping aboard his solar powered 'Go Anywhere Anytime' Chaseboard – Willey's favourite way of travelling around the cobbled streets of Trickletown.

He was in training for the Trickletown Valleys' Games, which was due to begin tomorrow morning. Willey was one of the best Chaseboard Challengers here in Trickletown. His Chaseboard could hover, glide, spin on its wheels or even surf on water and a voice-activated control box allowed him to control his Chaseboard with ease.

Solar powered 'Go Anywhere Anytime' Chaseboard

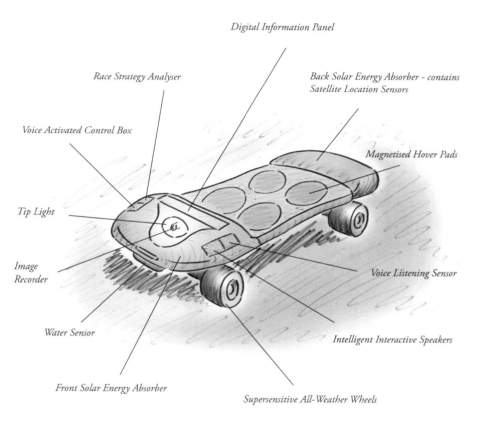

Digital Information Panel

Race Strategy Analyser

Back Solar Energy Absorber - contains Satellite Location Sensors

Voice Activated Control Box

Magnetised Hover Pads

Tip Light

Image Recorder

Voice Listening Sensor

Water Sensor

Intelligent Interactive Speakers

Front Solar Energy Absorber

Supersensitive All-Weather Wheels

Willey spent the morning looking for clues, but it wasn't until some time later when he returned to the deserted trail of Lock Street that he noticed something curious. 'The Key Stone!' thought Willey, pausing briefly before circling around a familiar granite rock. Now that his separate memories were back together, he was beginning to remember it!

Suddenly four of his fiercest Chaseboard rivals, Zack, Toya, Mitch and Maldon (four of the six notorious Cubonyento cousins) came to a shuddering halt beside him. They lived in Indigo Street – the current holder of the Trickletown Valleys' Games' 'Grand Trophy' – and they were all determined to retain it. Willey became slightly anxious, as two of the cousins were missing! – Malak and Jala. Where could they be hiding? They usually stick together. Something was certainly not right, but for the moment Willey had no more time to worry about it.

"CHASEBOARD CHALLENGE, GET SET!" shouted Toya. This set any Chaseboard within earshot to STANDBY.

Willey knew exactly what this challenge was all about. It was a cunning way to knock him down the Challenge Rankings before the Trickletown Valleys' Games the following morning, thus giving him little or no chance of winning the Chaseboard Challenge Trophy for Orange Street.

As soon as the challenge command was given the challenger's tip light turned green and the lights on all the other Chaseboards flash to amber. There was then a three second delay before the challenge began, and each vital second was marked by a short, sharp BEEP.

"Manual One Hover," instructed Willey.

BEEP.

"Best of luck Willey What'Nott," snarled Zack, his fiercest rival. He was obviously up to no good, so Willey would need to be careful.

BEEP.

The third and final beep was louder than the rest and signalled the Challenge to begin.

"BYE BYE WILLEY!" shouted Toya, immediately swinging her Chaseboard around and taking the race in the opposite direction.

"Unlucky Willey What'Nott, catch us if you can!" cried Mitch, who together with the others was now about ten board lengths ahead of him.

The Cubonyentos were heading to Indigo Street.

"CHASEBOARD CHALLENGE, GET SET!" shouted Toya. *This command set any Chaseboard within earshot to STANDBY.*

Although in hover mode, Willey's wheels sparked as they spun over the indigo-coloured cobbles of Trophy Bridge, where four defiant faces turned to smile at him, encouraging him to notice the Trickletown Valleys' Games' Grand Trophy. But unlike his opponents, Willey had noticed a cart load of laundry, inching its way around a fast approaching corner. You have never seen such a calamitous commotion, but despite this and many obstructions hidden around every corner, Willey found it difficult to move up any nearer to the leader of the Challenge. It was time for a change of tactics.

"MANUAL BOOST!" instructed Willey; this moved him up into second position. By the time they had climbed to the top of Indigo Hamlet, the Challenge was almost over. Zack had taken the lead, and it appeared to be a straightforward race to Indigo Basin.

"SONIC THRUST!" commanded Willey, crouching down with confidence on his speeding Chaseboard, in pursuit of Zack.

This was a big mistake! Zack and the others dived through a narrow open gateway, leaving Willey on a lonely course to Indigo Basin. Willey was moving too fast to follow and by the time he had swung his Chaseboard round, the gate was firmly closed. And behind it were the two missing cousins, Malak and Jala.

"PSSST!" one of his mum and dad's movement sensor, 'memory-loss' air fresheners was nailed to the gate post. If only Willey had known what these mysterious sprays were doing, he might just have been a little more careful.

Willey had lost, and all he could do was watch his Chaseboard ranking indicator slump to sixth.

"Unlucky Willey What'Nott," chuckled the Cubonyentos. "It appears you're not the Chaseboard racer you hoped you were!"

Willey was disappointed, of course, but he didn't let things worry him for long, and by the time he arrived back on Inner Street, his thoughts had returned to the mystery of the forgotten Key Stone.

Willey's wheels sparked as they spun over the indigo-coloured cobbles of Trophy Bridge – he noticed the Trickletown Valleys' Games' 'Grand Trophy'.

"Willey! WILLEY! Wait up! I have an important delivery for you!" Someone was shouting at him. It was Ivor Sack'Full, Trickletown's postman, frantically peddling towards him, waving an orange envelope. "Glad I caught you," panted Ivor. "This looks important. I found it hiding in my sack whilst I was cleaning it out at the post office."

Willey was pleased to see it, as it looked like the orange envelope that had delivered his mysterious circus ticket!

"Thanks Ivor," said Willey. "Auto Two, and make it snappy!"

Returning to the Key Stone, Willey slid his finger beneath the envelope's sticky surface; he felt the paper ripple and, without any further help from Willey, the envelope revealed its contents. A neatly written letter unfolded itself in his hands.

"Willey.

Time is very short!" The envelope said, reading out Willey's letter.

"You must find the Talking Teapot and visit the Knick-Knack Tree together. There Knicky-Knacky will help you and explain what must be done. To find the Talking Teapot you must consult the Trickletown Time Model, displayed in Blue Street Town Hall.

Be careful who you trust, as the forces working against you will be watching and could be hiding around any corner.

There are dangerous cans of spray marked 'air freshener' dotted all over Trickletown, you must do your best to avoid them, as they are causing all the Fuddles to loose their memories.

Good Luck Willey
'Signed' Q-O-F (Queen of Fuddles)

PS the Talking Teapot's nickname is Teabags. You may need to use it in order to convince him you are here to help."

"Willey! WILLEY! Wait up! I have an important delivery for you!" It was Ivor Sack'Full, Trickletown's postman, frantically peddling towards him, waving an orange envelope.

Fascinated by these words, Willey felt the nerves in his arms start to tingle. His adventure had really begun, and also something rather worrying had been brought to his attention. "The Knick-Knack Tree!" gasped Willey.

How had he managed to forget about something so magnificent? It appeared that the 'memory-loss' sprays were already beginning to work on him! Willey would need to be extra careful.

Willey looked towards the Emerald Forest, but all he could see was mist.

'The Mists of Time,' thought Willey. They were lingering low on the mountains and were hiding the Knick-Knack Tree's home; perhaps they had even captured it! Worried by this discovery and the other curious things which were happening, Willey sat on a tuft of grass and began to think …

Suddenly the sun's light dimmed and a dark shadowy shape formed over him. Willey had no time to react as a brown feathered bird swooped down and tore the letter from his fingertips, leaving behind a torn strip of paper with the Teapot's nickname on it. It disappeared so quickly that Willey feared that the secrets of his adventure had been stolen before it had really had a chance to begin!

A large grubby hand was placed on his shoulder.

"Aahh! … HELP!" Willey shouted, almost jumping out of his skin.

"Shush! Don't be alarmed," whispered the deep, recognisable voice of Phil Dug'It. To Willey's relief it was his best mate Eddy's dad. "Is there anything I can do to help?"

Mr Dug'It glanced around the edges of The Gambit in case anyone else was watching. Willey hesitated. The letter had warned him to be careful and he knew that if you ever told Mr Dug'It anything it was not very long before he told it to someone else.

Willey had no time to react as a brown feathered bird swooped and tore the letter from his fingertips. It seemed that the secrets of his adventure had been stolen before it had really had a chance to begin!

"Let's get you home," said Mr Dug'It, leading Willey back to Keystone Cottage and in through the open front door.

"Only us!" he shouted, but there was no reply. The cottage appeared empty.

"Park yourself here," said Mr Dug'It, pointing to one of the chairs by the kitchen table. He glanced into the living room, wandered back down the hallway and paused at the bottom of the winding wooden staircase.

PSSST! came a noise from another of those 'memory-loss' air fresheners; it made them jump.

"Willey, listen up …"

Willey did listen up because he was intrigued to know what Mr Dug'It might tell him. Mr Dug'It was now sitting opposite him at the kitchen table and Willey had to lean forward to hear him. "I think I have an idea of what you are up to, and if I can, I would like to help."

Willey was taken aback, as he hadn't been expecting an offer of help. He thought very carefully before answering Mr Dug'It's questions, as he did not want to give away all his secrets.

"Is there anything you are particularly looking for?"

"Have you lost anything?"

"Is there anything you would like me to dig up?"

The last request was no surprise, as Mr Dug'It never missed the opportunity to do some digging! He smiled hopefully across the table. There was an awkward and rather lengthy silence as Willey considered his reply.

"Be careful who you trust," the Orange Envelope had said, *"as the forces working against you will be watching and could be hiding around any corner!"*

'Surely Mr Dug'It must have seen the bird fly away with part of my letter,' thought Willey, 'and if he hadn't, why did he ask so many searching questions?' Phil Dug'It was a friend of the family and Willey's best mate's dad, so if he couldn't trust him who could he trust?

Mr Dug'It paused at the bottom of the winding wooden staircase. PSSST! came a noise from another of those 'memory-loss' air fresheners; it made them jump. The house appeared empty!

All things carefully considered, Willey decided that he might need some help so he told Mr Dug'It everything, except for his journey beneath the circus tent and the Talking Teapot's nickname – just in case Mr Dug'It was not as friendly as he appeared, or anyone else was listening!

After another lengthy pause, the silence was broken when Mr Dug'It almost choked on the Knick-Knack Nut biscuit he had just helped himself to. His coughing prompted clattering footsteps and in walked the *fading* figures of Mr and Mrs What'Nott. Neither of them explained where they had come from – in fact, they had been hiding at the top of the stairs in an attempt to find out what Willey and Phil Dug'It might be up to.

Mr and Mrs What'Nott together with the two unfortunate Mr Got-a-Lott's were gradually disappearing. The Mists of Time were taking over their bodies and soon they may disappear completely.

"There you are Willey! Thanks for bringing him back, Phil," they said politely, at the same time.

"No problem," coughed and spluttered Phil, whilst Mrs What'Nott poured him a glass of water and Mr What'Nott tried to piece together the fragments of the conversation across the kitchen table. Coughing and spluttering again, Mr Dug'It, unable to speak, left the cottage. PSSST! went the 'memory-loss' air freshener again, spraying him as he went.

Willey held his breath and attempted to follow.

"Oh no you don't, Willey What'Nott! It's time for lunch, and you are not going out till you have finished every bit of it," said his mother sternly.

"What you need to remember about Phil Dug'It," concluded Mr What'Nott, "is that he can't be trusted with anything …"

- Chapter 7 -

It's the Talking Teapot!

"To find the Talking Teapot you must consult the Trickletown Time Model displayed in Blue Street Town Hall." That's what the Orange Envelope had said.

"You must find the Talking Teapot and together visit the Knick-Knack Tree. Here Knicky-Knacky will help you and explain what must be done."

Hidden within the innermost chambers of Blue Street Town Hall was one of Trickletown's greatest treasures: 'The Trickletown Time Model. The model was so much more than just a means of finding your way around Trickletown Valleys' Crater. It was three dimensional in shape and it could demonstrate different time zones; looking with exceptional detail into the past, the present and the future. It tracked every living thing in Trickletown Valley's Crater and would indicate to others where you were if you ever got lost in time.

When the Fuddles first arrived here, the Crater was a dangerous place. The Mists of Time were battling to take control, and when the Fuddles entered the Mists they were often never seen again. There was no map or model to help them, so after much deliberation the Trickletown Committee decided to do something about it. They ordered a large amount of Replicating Clay and set about making the Trickletown Time Model.

Work was soon under way, creating every house, tree, stream and landmark. Finally, the model was complete and became the living, beating heart of Trickletown.

By this time, the innermost chambers of Blue Street Town Hall and the Trickletown Time Model had virtually been forgotten – the 'memory-loss' spray had done its work and as Willey approached the Time Model there were no Fuddles to be seen. Willey walked up and stood on a green, glowing platform and placed his fingers in the slot provided. The model even had its own voice, soft and reassuring: "Welcome Willey, my records tell me that this is your first official visit to the Time Model; would you like any help?"

The control panel flashed to attract his attention.

"Umm, no thank you," replied Willey after reading the instructions in front of him, which simply said "ENTER REQUEST".

Taking care to spell each word correctly, Willey did just that:

I wish to find the Talking Teapot, he typed.

Willey pressed the confirmation button and eagerly looked towards the model for a reply. The model was alive. Willey could see the shadowy figures of Fuddles moving in front of him. Even a line of clouds drifted over the model's position.

A green light blinked in the centre of the Time Model, inside the ring of oak trees at the centre of The Gambit. Willey looked puzzled. He repeated his request again, just in case he had made a mistake, but the green light blinked in exactly the same position. Willey studied the information on the screen in front of him and then realised to his surprise that the location of the Talking Teapot had been requested earlier by none other than Mr Phil Dug'It!

The soft, reassuring voice spoke again: "Your request has been successfully completed. Do you have any questions?"

"No thanks," said Willey, tapping the screen where it said "TOUCH TO EXIT". He was now in such a hurry to leave that he was half-way down the corridor when he heard the voice again. "Please follow the exit signs and close the door on your way out. Thank you."

'I wish to find the Talking Teapot,' *he typed. Willey pressed the confirmation button and eagerly looked towards the model for a reply.*

Once outside, Willey wasted no time in returning to The Gambit and arrived very quickly, thanks to the speed of his solar-powered street bike.

When Willey reached the spot of the Talking Teapot's location, he found a large crowd gathering. To his dismay Phil Dug'It had beaten him to it and there were already several deep holes around the area – Phil Dug'It was the centre of attention, and causing quite a commotion.

Ignoring everyone, Phil continued to dig, until finally …

CLUNK!

All the bickering stopped. Something was definitely there, and it was not very long before everyone realised what it was!

"It's the Talking Teapot!" everyone said together.

This was not a welcome discovery. The appearance of the Talking Teapot jogged the Fuddles' memories and they began to remember the story the *nasty* Mr What'Nott had told them – that the Talking Teapot was to blame for the disappearance of The Million Wiggle Fish Pond.

But the Talking Teapot was innocent; it was the Mists of Time who were causing trouble. Mr What'Nott had lied about everything, and his 'made-up story' went something like this …

"It happened on a dark and stormy night when a mischievous comet called Climaticus was circling the Earth. The Mysterious Mists of Time were swirling around and the Talking Teapot was helping me secure the Million Wiggle Fish Pond beneath The Gambit. I was just about to secure the Key in place with the Emerald Ring when suddenly, and without warning, the Talking Teapot stole the Hour Glass Key and snatched the Emerald Ring from my fingers. He then ran away with them both into the Mists of Time. The Rainbow Fish followed, as it of course was their duty to protect the Hour Glass Key, but they never returned."

From that day onwards, the Million Wiggle Fish Pond, the Hour Glass Key, and the Talking Teapot were never seen or spoken about again.

CLUNK!
All the bickering stopped. Something was definitely there, and Willey had a pretty
good idea what it was!
"It's the Talking Teapot!" everyone said together.

Mr Dug'It, whether he intended to or not, disappeared head first into the hole, leaving a pair of wobbly legs for all to see …

"HELP! Get me out of here – I've got it!" cried a muffled voice, deep in the bottom of the hole.

Taking control of the situation, the Mayor of Trickletown, Lord William Watch'Over, shooed everyone away from the hole. Pointing to the Cubonyento Brothers, who were big and strong, he bellowed, "When I count down from THREE I want you to pull him up and out of there!"

They did as they were asked and bent over to grab what they could of Mr Dug'It.

"THREE! TWO! ONE!" shouted everyone. "PULL!"

They knew the Cubonyento Brothers were strong, but not this strong! Mr Dug'It was catapulted into the air from the hole and flew right out of his trousers! He was caught by the crowd – but the Talking Teapot soared high up to the edge of the atmosphere and then began to fall!

"Catch it!" everyone cried.

The Cubonyento Brothers held out Mr Dug'It's trousers – on which it bounced – and when the Talking Teapot eventually landed, it fell into Lord William Watch'Over's arms!

The Mayor stood very still, not daring to move but nothing happened, so he lifted the Teapot's lid and looked inside … then he peered down the Teapot's spout for signs of a blockage … and then he waited for any sign of life … there was still nothing happening, so he tapped the Teapot's body.

"Perhaps he's dead!" shouted someone from the crowd.

Mr Dug'It was catapulted into the air from the hole and flew right out of his trousers! The Talking Teapot soared high up to the edge of the atmosphere and then it began to fall.

The Mayor was just about to tap the Teapot again when … *suddenly* … a pair of eyes opened on the Teapot's body, making everyone jump. The Teapot fell to the ground and bounced, but before it could bounce again, two teapot-sized arms and legs sprang out from the Teapot's body and it started to run!

It dived between legs and it ran over shoulders. It was chased into Key Stone Cottage and out the other side, over the large Granite Key Stone and down a shallow stream. By the time it had reached the edge of Inner Street, there was nobody left standing to chase it. The last of those brave enough to try was Phil Dug'It and he ended up sitting in the stream, wearing just a pair of spotty green underpants.

The Talking Teapot was gone and Willey needed to go after it. He was getting back on his bike when his best mate Eddy Dug'It whizzed past him, riding his own metallic green street bike.

"We have to go after the Teapot, Willey!" shouted Eddy." I knew my dad was up to something – he never goes out in such a hurry unless he has something to dig up!"

The Teapot fell to the ground and bounced, but before it could bounce again, two teapot-sized arms and legs sprang out from the Teapot's body and it started to run!

The Talking Teapot's trail led up the Emerald Pathway to the Emerald Forest; the forgotten home of the Knick-Knack Tree. The Pathway was not easy to follow – it was littered with fallen trees and rocks in an attempt to *stop* anyone from following it – but this made the ride even more exciting as the boys continued their race to the edge of the Mist. There was very little sign of the Teapot – only the occasional footprint to let them know they were on the right track.

The light was beginning to fade and although the boys were keen to find the Talking Teapot, the Mysterious Mists of Time were closing in and tugging at the wheels of their street bikes. Eddy skidded to a halt.

"It's no good Willey, the Mists are getting too thick and I daren't go on any further. Dad was desperate to ask the Teapot lots of questions but it looks like they will all have to wait."

Willey stopped too. He had wondered why Eddy was so keen to chase after the Teapot and was now considering what questions Mr Dug'It was hoping to ask. His thoughts were interrupted by Eddy shouting, "Come on Willey, the Got-a-Lott Museum! We have to get hold of a Time-Line!"

Eddy was right. The only safe way to enter the Mists of Time was to use a Time-Line and the only place where they knew they would find one was in the halls of the Got-a-Lott Museum.

The Talking Teapot's trail led up the Emerald Pathway towards the forgotten location of the Knick-Knack Tree. The Pathway was not easy to follow — it was littered with fallen trees and rocks.

- Chapter 8 -

In Search of a Time-Line

'Time-Lines' are instruments used to travel through time. They consist of a Gold and Silver Ring and between the rings is a rainbow of light. All that Fuddles needed to do to travel through time was to leave the Gold Ring behind and take the Silver Ring with them. To return, they just look back over their shoulder and follow the rainbow back to the Gold Ring.

WOW! Trickletown's Labyrinths – the very mention of the word "Labyrinth" in Trickletown Valleys' Crater would set your heart thumping. And beneath the Crater there were seven of them, one below each of Trickletown's colourful hamlets. The Labyrinths were not just a glorious tangle of underground tunnels. They had minds of their own and if you ever had cause to enter one, you would need to keep your wits about you as they were dangerous places.

Willey and Eddy were heading for Yellow Street Labyrinth, as this was the secret way in to the Got-a-Lott Museum. And no matter how dangerous it was, they were desperate to get hold of a Time-Line to help them search for the Talking Teapot.

The boys hid their bikes in some bushes and tiptoed beneath an arch of the Yellow River Bridge. Above them they could hear the sounds of Fuddles' feet and chattering about the Teapot's Grand Escape.

"Do you think it knows we are here?" whispered Eddy.

The boys hid their bikes in some bushes and tiptoed beneath an arch of the Yellow River Bridge.

The boys were looking for any sign of the Labyrinth's tunnel. But unless it was ready to show itself, they might not even spot it.

"Look," whispered Willey, pointing across the river to a disturbance on the opposite bank. "There – between the boulders!"

Willey was right; the entrance to Yellow Street Labyrinth was beginning to open. And across the surface of the river a pathway of stepping stones magically appeared.

"Come on Eddy, we need to be quick!" urged Willey, leading the way.

The two boys sprinted over the stones and headed straight for the growing tunnel entrance. It never stayed open for long, so as soon as they reached it they dived straight in. The entrance to the Labyrinth closed directly behind them and the stones across the surface of the river quickly disappeared.

Once inside the boys noticed nothing particularly special about the tunnel; after all it was only performing its official Labyrinth duties. The way ahead was lit by a series of tunnel lights and along the tunnel walls were many piles of 'This & That'. *('This & That' is Fuddle terminology for any old rubbish!)*

Anything which a Fuddle no longer needed, or was broken beyond repair, would be discarded down one of the many 'This & That' pipes dotted around Trickletown Valleys' Crater. Things ended up piled along the edges of the tunnel walls until the staff from the Got-a-Lott Museum arrived to sort them out. They took with them things the museum did not already have or might find a very good use for. Then at one minute to five every day, anything left behind was washed away in what was known as the 'Big Flush', into the furnace at the bottom of Indigo Basin. The Big Flush was a wave of water, rushing out from the underground Emerald Lake. It only lasted for one minute – and then, precisely on the stroke of 5 o'clock, a spiralling ring of hot steam shot out of the top of Indigo Basin with a BOOM!

"Look," whispered Willey, "There between the boulders!"
Willey was right; the entrance to Yellow Street Labyrinth was beginning to open.
And across the surface of the river a pathway of stepping stones magically appeared.

So if you did happen to be in any of the Labyrinths at around that time of day you had better start planning your escape.

SPLOSH! Willey ducked but Eddy didn't and was covered in a surge of dirty dish water. There were no pipes to be seen; the Labyrinth could squirt out anything, whenever it needed.

"Bother that tunnel!" grumbled Eddy, who was given a second soaking just for complaining!

"There!" said Willey suddenly, as they continued down the tunnel. "There's the iron ladder to the Got-a-Lott Museum!"

Eddy was really pleased to see it. "Up or down?" he enquired. It was either up to the public galleries or down into the Museum basement.

"Down," was Willey's reply, but as he said it, the Labyrinth's tunnel began to rumble.

Everything up till now had been going exactly to plan, except perhaps for Eddy's drenching. But their trip inside Yellow Street Labyrinth was about to get a whole lot worse! The slimy yellow toads began tightening their grip on the tunnel walls, and squeezing between the cracks in the floor – the mysterious Mists of Time were about to cause trouble.

"Quick Eddy, grab hold of the ladder!" Willey shouted urgently – but he was too late. The last available exits were closing fast and there was only just time for the tunnel bats to fly out to safety. Willey looked anxiously at his watch. He could not believe it – the hands were speeding up and the time was approaching 5 o'clock!

"THE BIG FLUSH!" he screamed as a blast of cool air rushed through the tunnel and a wave of murky green water swept them off their feet.

Willey looked anxiously at his watch. He couldn't believe it – the hands were speeding up and the time was approaching 5 o'clock!
"THE BIG FLUSH!" he screamed as a blast of cool air rushed through the tunnel and a wave of murky water swept them off their feet.

The boys took a large gulp of air as the water engulfed them but after a few seconds they surfaced. Willey grabbed a half-deflated football and Eddy clung to the remains of a garden bench, in an attempt to keep afloat. At least they were still alive, and once they had acclimatised to their surroundings, the ride seemed quite exciting!

The Labyrinth launched them out over the Trickletown rivers.

"Green River … Blue River …" Willey whispered their names as the Labyrinth's tunnels spat them out and sucked them in again.

Then came the worrying sound of water squirting down Indigo Tunnel! They knew the excitement of the ride was all but over. Suddenly, there was silence, and the deafening rush of the water all but disappeared. They were falling, and falling fast … into the bottomless, fiery belly of Indigo Basin and they could not stop! They feared there was no way out, but just as a cauldron of steam erupted back from the heat of the furnace, the Labyrinth's mouth appeared in the basin walls and sucked them out.

With a loud squelchy SSLLUUCCKK, and in a matter of moments, they were dumped into the Museum basement, closely followed by several items of 'This & That'.

"Ouch!" said Willey, as the half-deflated football hit him in the chest. Eddy braced himself for the arrival of the garden bench – which thankfully never appeared! A warm breath of air from the Labyrinth dried them off – and in the distance they heard Indigo Basin go BOOM.

"Boy, that was close!" said Willey looking at his watch.

It was second nature for everyone to look at their watch when they heard Indigo Basin go BOOM. Everyone set their clocks by it. But this time, instead of the hands on Willey's watch moving forward, they began to move back. The Mysterious Mists of Time were no longer around to cause trouble; so Time could return to where it should be, and it was only 3 o'clock.

They were falling, and falling fast … into the bottomless, fiery belly of Indigo Basin. They feared there was no way out, but just as there seemed to be no escape from the cauldron of steam, the Labyrinth's mouth appeared in the basin walls and sucked them out.

"All this trouble for a Time-Line," whispered Eddy, nudging Willey forwards and round the corner. They had clambered up a set of stone steps into the Got-a-Lott Museum and were now at the end of a corridor full of doorways to the Museum offices.

"Quiet!" whispered Willey, creeping as close as he could to the edge of the wall and ducking beneath each of the windows. Most of the doors were closed but as they neared the end of the corridor they could hear the sound of voices. Willey was startled to hear his own name mentioned!

"If we can't catch him today, we will lock him in his bedroom tonight!" said one of the voices.

"Yes indeed, he must be stopped," said another.

"Certainly before the Trickletown Valleys' Games have a chance to begin."

Willey was sure he knew who all the voices belonged to: it was his *villainous* mum and dad and Mr Got-a-Lott, the Museum's owner. Willey also remembered him as the large round Ticket Collector from the circus! As Willey began to consider why they were here, one of the doors swung open and out into the corridor walked the somewhat transparent figure of Mr Got-a-Lott.

"Quiet!" whispered Willey, creeping as close as he could to the edge of the wall and ducking beneath each of the windows.

Before Willey and Eddy had a chance to hide Mr Got-a-Lott turned around and saw them. "CATCH THEM!" he bellowed. "CATCH THEM HOWEVER YOU CAN!"

Eddy was not fast enough and was caught in an instant.

Willey was far too quick. He ran towards the Museum storerooms.

"STOP HIM, STOP THAT BOY!" Mr Got-a-Lott bellowed again, his face as red as a tomato.

But Willey was up for the chase and, like the Talking Teapot's grand escape on The Gambit, he was more than up to the challenge.

Eventually Willey reached the Alley he was looking for – the 'A to Z' Alley. It was quiet, with not a Fuddle to be seen between him and what he was after. Willey sprinted from A to P, then skidded from Q to T, before diving into the box marked 'Time-Lines'. As soon as his hand lay upon one, he was out of there fast, through the Museum entrance, over Yellow River Bridge and back to his bike. Only then did he glance around to see if Eddy had managed to escape. He hadn't. Willey pressed the solar energy burst button on his street bike and headed back up the Emerald Pathway.

Eventually Willey reached the Alley he was looking for – the 'A to Z' Alley. It was quiet, with not a Fuddle in sight. Willey sprinted from A to P, then skidded from Q to T, before diving into the box marked 'Time-Lines'. As soon as his hand lay upon one, he was out of there fast.

- Chapter 9 -

A Brief Encounter by a Fence

The weather was beginning to deteriorate and it had started to drizzle.

It was far too dangerous for a street bike: there were too many obstacles in the way – and now he was approaching the Mists of Time, Willey would need to be extra careful.

He hid his bike and the Golden Ring of his Time-Line deep in some bushes. He was now even more determined to find the Talking Teapot, just as the Orange Envelope had said. So with the Silver Ring of his Time-Line safely on his finger, he continued his journey on foot and disappeared into the thick, grey mist.

Ahead of him lay the Emerald Forest and the mysteriously forgotten location of the Knick-Knack Tree.

Willey wondered what he might find there, as in his dream he had seen the Knick-Knack Tree's face, and it was surrounded by thorns!

The rain was falling heavily now and there was no further sign of the Talking Teapot. Willey was about to give up, when his thoughts were rudely interrupted by a loud shout: "WATCH OUT WHERE YOU ARE TREADING! And if I were standing where you are, I would not take another step nearer that fence!"

Willey could not see anyone, and he hadn't noticed a fence, even though he was now standing right in front of one.

"Colonel Tuft, 455 Regiment, Trickletown Valleys' Under-Cover Grass Army, at your service!" shouted the voice. "I am here to warn you about the dangers of Cedric's Field."

Willey listened intently as Colonel Tuft continued with what was worrying information, "You do not want to enter that field, it is far too dangerous," whispered Colonel Tuft, making sure he could not be overheard. "Even if you manage to get past the Field Grass Army, there is Cedric to worry about … and then if you get past him there is the hedge of venomous thorns …"

This information was certainly alarming, but whilst Willey was taking it in, he realised he had a question of his own for Colonel Tuft; wherever he might be hiding!

"Have you seen the Talking Teapot?" asked Willey.

"Teabags?" replied the voice. "Yes he was around here earlier, but didn't stay long. He was muttering something about a lawnmower and said he would be back first thing in the morning."

SPLOSH! Willey slipped backwards and sat in a puddle.

Colonel Tuft laughed. Willey could now see the fence and it was HUGE; and on a gate that was bigger than a bus were the words:

'CEDRIC'S FIELD

KEEP OUT

PS Keep off the Grass'

'Well, if this is the size of the gate,' thought Willey, he was not entirely sure he wanted to meet Cedric at all.

Colonel Tuft and his Under-Cover Grass Army manoeuvred into position around Willey sitting in the puddle.

Although they were all extremely small and made of grass, they were very well-armed with an impressive display of weaponry. Headed by a sharp and fearsome blade on the tip of their rifles, and beneath a line of tin hats appeared a row of Fuddle-like faces.

A sternly raised eyebrow was enough to bring this fearless rank of soldiers to attention.

"Captain Couch-Grass – SIR!"

"Sergeant Dog's-Tail – SIR!"

"Corporal Hay-Maker – SIR!"

"Privates Timothy, Foxtail, Cock's-Foot and Flattergrass;"

"Sir", "Sir", "Sir", "Sir"; "Pickle Sir!"

"'Pickle Sir!' Who the … Oh it's … Well the impertinence of it!" shouted Colonel Tuft.

Colonel Tuft and his Under-Cover Grass Army manoeuvred into position around Willey sitting in the puddle. Although they were all extremely small and made of grass, they were very well-armed with an impressive display of weaponry.

"Interrupting my parade! Can't you hop away and annoy somebody else?"

The intruder was a smartly dressed Rainbow-hopper called 'Pickle', renowned for his sudden appearances and the magic tricks he liked to play on Colonel Tuft, especially when he was performing his official duties.

"WATCH OUT! THERE'S A CAT!" shouted Pickle, scaring the wits out of everyone including Willey, who was still extremely worried about Cedric.

Colonel Tuft froze to the spot! He was petrified of cats. However, in this particular instance it was only one of Pickle's magic spells and Pickle shouted out the rest of it –

"WATCH OUT! THERE'S A CAT!

Well fancy that! Turn over Colonel Tuft's tin hats!"

*** 'PUFF' ***

There was of course no cat to be seen, but the spell worked perfectly and the helmets of Colonel Tuft's grass soldiers turned upside-down.

It was Willey's turn to laugh. By the time they had turned them back, their helmets had filled up with water and everyone was in line for a drenching.

The spell worked perfectly and the helmets of Colonel Tuft's grass soldiers turned upside-down.

Suddenly forked lightning flashed over the Emerald Causeway and four giant bales of bull nuts (presumably food for Cedric!) catapulted over the fence. In an instant, everyone had gone! Willey was on his own.

Whoever Cedric might be, he must be dangerous – for if Willey's thoughts of Cedric were not enough to scare him, on the other side of the fence, in Cedric's Field, the colossal Field Grass Army was busy maneuvering itself into position. Hundreds of thousands of grass-like soldiers quickly formed a formidable barrier – not only to keep Willey out of the field, but to keep Cedric away from the fence.

If Willey was going to attempt the journey across Cedric's Field it would not be easy. As he wondered what to do next, a shadowy shape appeared above him and dropped the Orange Envelope into his hands. Excitedly, Willey tucked it into his pocket and made a run for it. He never looked back; he just followed the Rainbow of Light back to the Golden Ring of his Time-Line and jumped on his bike.

*Suddenly forked lightning flashed over the Emerald Causeway and four giant bales
of bull nuts catapulted over the fence. In an instant, everyone had gone!*

- Chapter 10 -

In-a-Pickle Farmyard

Willey had hardly slept. The words in his latest Orange Letter were going over and over in his mind.

Be at the gateway to Cedric's Field tomorrow morning, before the cock has time to crow. Tell no one where you are going and bring nobody with you.

Signed
Q-O-F (The Queen of Fuddles)"

If Willey had said these words once, he had repeated them a hundred times. He certainly could not wait to see the first rays of sunlight burst over the mountain tops, triggering the trumpeting blasts of Brown Bottom (Farmer Crisp's cockerel) into the cauldron of Trickletown Valleys' Crater.

Willey had spent the night in the bike shed, hiding in a pile of old sacks. It was far too dangerous to stay in his bedroom, now he knew that his mum and dad were trying to capture him.

He pulled the pile of sacks tightly round his body. It was cold in the bike shed and there was nothing else around to keep him warm.

A narrow chink of light was beginning to appear above the top of the door. He should soon be on his way up the Emerald Pathway and back to the giant gate into Cedric's Field, as the Orange Envelope had told him – but the night had been a long one, Willey had hardly slept, and now that it was time to get up he could feel himself falling asleep.

Willey had spent the night in the bike shed, hiding in a pile of old sacks.

Meanwhile, and not so very far away, on the edge of Red Street and at the centre of In-a-Pickle Farm, the Talking Teapot yawned and stretched his legs. He had spent the night hiding in a hole in Big Bale Barn and was now extremely pleased it was time to get up. He too had been planning his return to Cedric's Field, but four of Farmer Crisp's plump, speckled hens were annoying him, scratching around in the dust, in search of their breakfast. They had now been joined by Brown Bottom, the splendid cockerel, who was noisily preparing his ascent to the top of a gatepost.

Teabags had had more than enough of it.

"SILENCE!" he shouted.

For a moment Brown Bottom and his four plump companions were startled into silence, but soon returned to their repetitious routines.

"OOOOO! HOOOO! HOOOO!" cried the Talking Teapot. "Haven't you chickens got anything better to do early in the mornings?"

Of course there was no reply, and of course they hadn't anything better to do, other than perhaps lay an egg and occasionally sit on it.

"STOP RIGHT WHERE YOU ARE!" ordered Teabags, heading for the water trough. These noisy chickens were in for a big surprise! They were going to listen to the Talking Teapot whether they liked it or not.

The Talking Teapot yawned and stretched his legs. He had spent the night hiding in a hole in Big Bale Barn and was now extremely pleased it was time to get up.

S P L A S H!

A great raft of water launched into the air. Following four complete lengths of underwater breaststroke, several prolonged bouts of blowing bubbles and numerous squirts of water in the direction of the chickens, the Talking Teapot surfaced and danced around the edge of the water trough, singing his favourite chicken song:

♫

"Chick, chick, chick, chick, chicken,
Lay a little egg for me.
Chick, chick, chick, chick, chicken,
I'd love one for my tea.
I haven't had an egg since I don't know when
So please lay one for me.
Yippee ..." ♫

before slipping backwards, back into the water.

The poor befuddled chickens could only cluck, as they watched the Teapot haul himself out and, with a belly full of water, wander in the direction of the dog house.

The dog house belonged to 'Fetch', Farmer Crisp's faithful, but lazy, bloodhound. He was currently where he liked to be first thing in the morning; chewing one of Farmer Crisp's slippers, by the side of Farmer Crisp's bed.

"There you are, my feathered friends," said the Talking Teapot, after dragging Fetch's dinner bowl into the centre of In-a-Pickle Farmyard, and filling it up with water from the end of his spout. "Take a drink of that and then let me know what you think of it."

S P L A S H!
A great raft of water launched into the air. The Talking Teapot surfaced and
danced around the edge of the water trough, singing his favourite chicken song.

Unknown to the unsuspecting chickens, drinking water from the Talking Teapot's spout would allow them to talk for one or two hours. The chickens just thought they were drinking a dish of cool water.

Brown Bottom and his four speckled hens continued to drink ...

Eventually one of the hens raised her head and looked around.

"What a wonderfully refreshing drink," she said.

Her friends were astounded. How could they know that drinking water from the Teapot's spout would make them talk? At that moment, Brown Bottom launched himself to the top of the gatepost.

His early morning duties were about to begin!

Brown Bottom fidgeted around in his position, taking care to cover the part of his un-feathered body which gave him his name, a feather-sparse, skinny brown bottom.

And then, when everything was ready, and everyone in the farmyard was prepared for a Cock-a-Doodly-Doo – Brown Bottom didn't 'crow'!

"WAKEY-WAKEY FOR HEAVEN'S SAKEY!" shouted Brown Bottom, at the top of his voice.

Milkshake the cow and Crunch the goat raised their heads from their munching, to watch the rest of this sparkling performance, and Brown Bottom did not disappoint.

"WAKEY-WAKEY, RISE AND SHINE;
MRS MERRY'FEATHER'S KNICKERS ARE HANGING ON HER LINE!"

shouted Brown Bottom. It was something he had always wanted to say.

"WAKEY-WAKEY FOR HEAVEN'S SAKEY!"
shouted Brown Bottom, at the top of his voice.

Milkshake and Crunch spat out the grassy cuds they had been chewing with such force that they cannoned into the hollow tin walls of Big Bale Barn: 'BOOM BOOM', one after the other.

The echoing 'BOOM BOOMS' continued for several moments and everyone looked up to Farmer Crisp's open bedroom window. If this hadn't been enough to wake him, nothing would.

Fetch was beginning to bark and, with a slipper primed and ready, Farmer Crisp appeared at the bedroom window.

"FETCH!" shouted Farmer Crisp, hurling a pink, rabbit slipper on a course to knock Brown Bottom clean off his gatepost, but then, as his beady eyes spotted the Talking Teapot his excitement increased.

"FETCH! FETCH! FETCH!" shouted Farmer Crisp.

"FETCH ME THAT TEA – " but before he could say "POT", Farmer Crisp was knocked out of his own bedroom window by an exuberant flying hound. Fetch thought his master had been calling him over for cuddles!

It did take quite some time for the dust to settle, but when it did: the hens were in the hen house; Brown Bottom was in the water trough; the Talking Teapot was nowhere to be seen; and Farmer Crisp was barely able to move, although his landing had been relatively soft – on a pile of bagged-up bull nuts. Luckily it was not the smelly heap of cow dung that had been there three days earlier!

Fetch growled; he had found Farmer Crisp's soggy slipper and was now extremely annoyed that his dinner bowl was not where it should be. However, he could not see anyone he could blame for moving it, so taking a well-earned drink of Teapot's 'magic water', he returned to his master.

"Here's your soggy slipper," said Fetch, "and don't say I never fetch anything for you. Now will you be in need of a nice warm blanket or do you think I should call for an ambulance?"

"FETCH!" shouted Farmer Crisp, hurling a pink, soggy slipper on a course to knock Brown Bottom clean off his gatepost, but then, as his beady eyes spotted the Talking Teapot, his excitement increased.

The Talking Teapot was on the move again, and everyone was on the look-out ...

There was a shout from high in the roof tops of Blue Street Town Hall: "TRIM the GARDENER'S RIVER VIEW ALLOTMENTS!"

The Talking Teapot had been spotted!

Word soon spread throughout Trickletown and before very long a crowd of excited Fuddles began to gather at the entrance to Green Street. Even those peering over Mrs Merry'Feather's hedge decided her knickers were not worth looking at and moved over to see what was happening.

This was their chance to catch the Talking Teapot and to find out what had happened to the Hour Glass Key! In no time at all, the entrance to Green Street was blocked by an impenetrable barrier, through which not even a mouse could have crossed. Anything and everything you might use to catch a Teapot had been brought along to help. There were boxes, hooks and nets and there were lassos, garden spades and forks, saucepans, fire guards, water pistols, water tanks, rubber fish ponds and even a bath tub! All of them lined up and ready to entrap the Talking Teapot. Not only that; behind this great assortment of objects and the line of Fuddles supporting them, stood an array of colourful banners, announcing the arrival of the Trickletown Valleys' Games the next morning.

Not far ahead could be heard the distant rumbling of an engine. It was coming from Trim the Gardener's tool shed! Teabags was up to something and it would not be very long before everyone found out what it was.

The doors to the shed burst open and out from the depths of the shadows shot a Gismo 500 lawnmower. Hanging on tight to its handle-bars was a triumphant Talking Teapot! With its blades at full tilt, this unstoppable machine sped swiftly over the vegetable patch. It made short work of the carrots before launching from the furrows of the potato bed and clipping the top of a topiary hedge – a family of skilfully cut partridges flew off in the process.

Undeterred by both takeoff and landing, the Talking Teapot hurtled down Green Street and headed for the barrier.

No one could believe what was happening. It appeared the unstoppable machine would plough into the impenetrable barrier, because although the Talking Teapot had managed to start this menacing mower, he had no idea how to stop it!

The crowd looked up and over the gleaming, green cobbles of Green Street, and the Talking Teapot stared wide-eyed at the fearsome barrier, and then, at the point of unavoidable disaster, came a noise which could possibly save them – the unmistakable sound of an ambulance, travelling at speed through the gates of Green Street Hospital.

There was only one thing to do: EVERYONE GOT OUT OF THE WAY.

Those who could, began to run, whilst others could only push. As they rolled and tripped and scattered, a gap began to form, just about big enough and just in time – Teabags drove straight through it, and guided the lawnmower on a straight destructive course across The Gambit. He was heading for the Emerald Pathway and the entrance to Cedric's Field.

The ambulance followed on through the open gap and turned down Inner Street, in the direction of In-a-Pickle Farm and to the rescue of poor old Farmer Crisp.

However, none of this was very good news for Willey, who was now asleep in his bike shed.

From the gates of Green Street Hospital, and moving at considerable speed,
came the unmistakable sight and sounds of an ambulance.
There was only one thing to do: EVERYONE GOT OUT OF THE WAY.

- Chapter 11 -

Cedric's Field

'*Willey,*
Be at the gateway to Cedric's field tomorrow morning, before the cock has time to crow,' the Orange Envelope had said.

Well the cock (which of course was Brown Bottom) had already crowed and Willey was nowhere to be seen.

Luckily Teabags was late, and now the sound of the noisy lawnmower was waking Willey up. He scrambled through the door of the bike shed, only to be greeted by a cloud of white smoke and the sight of the Talking Teapot, whistling past him.

"STOP!" shouted Willey, but the lawnmower was stopping for no one.

"TEABAGS! TEABAGS! TEABAGS! I HAVE TO COME WITH YOU, TO THE KNICK-KNACK TREE!" shouted Willey.

This appeared to do the trick. The lawnmower swung around Key Stone Cottage, giving Willey the chance to catch up.

"YA'Heeeee! YA'Haaaaa! YA'Hooooo!" shouted Willey, as he jumped aboard the contraption. It was as if he was riding a race horse and was heading over the gallops. In fact, he had just burnt his bottom on a very hot engine.

The chaos left behind them was now of little consequence, as the clatter of the engine and whirring of the cutters marked their climb up the Emerald Pathway. The mysterious Mists of Time soon started to thicken and it was not very long before the gate into Cedric's Field loomed large in front of them.

Willey's heart missed a beat as the giant gate swung open. The lock had been successfully picked by Colonel Tuft, who proudly saluted his success from the top of the gatepost.

Willey's eyes searched around Cedric's Field. He was sure the way ahead was going to be dangerous and he was right. Manoeuvring into position was the mean and menacing Field Grass Army; hundreds of thousands of blades were pointing back at them. Willey could hear the shouts of the army generals commanding their soldiers and, as if this was not enough, the menacing silhouette of a giant bull appeared on the horizon. Whoever it was trying to stop them from reaching the Knick-Knack Tree had made a good job of it – and now Cedric, the guardian of the field was almost upon them!

Willey's heart missed a beat as the giant gate swung open. The lock had been successfully picked by Colonel Tuft, who proudly saluted his success from the top of the gatepost.

"Willey! Take off your jacket!" shouted Teabags, guiding the Gismo 500 through the open gateway into attack.

Slivers of grass flew everywhere; bayonets and boots and helmets rained from the heavens; the magnificent Field Grass Army was no match for the blades of the lawnmower.

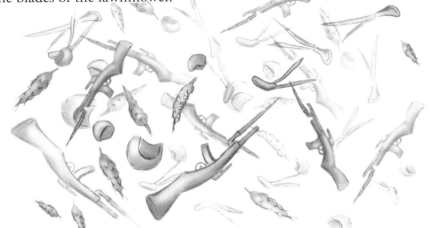

"Get yourself ready, Willey. When I give the command, raise your jacket and lean back on the lawnmower!"

Willey braced himself. Cedric's huge, fearsome figure was now so close it blotted out the sky. His eyes were blood-red; his horns menacing; his head low and ready to charge – and this giant armoured ox (an aurochs) was heading straight for them!

"NOW!" cried the Talking Teapot.

As Willey's bright red jacket flew high in the air, Cedric raised his head. The lawnmower zoomed beneath him, clipping the hair down his soft under-belly and as they appeared from this difficult task, the lawnmower cut off the tip of Cedric's tail!

Cedric launched himself into the air – his bellows loud enough to reach the streets of Trickletown. Then as he danced a painful jig around the field, the last that anyone saw of him was the glow of his freshly clipped parts, disappearing into the mist.

With a CLATTER and a BANG and a BUMP, the Gismo 500 lawnmower crashed into a living bank of thorns and came to rest against the trunk of a large, yet familiar tree!

As Willey's bright red jacket flew high in the air, Cedric raised his head.
The lawnmower zoomed beneath him, clipping the hair down his soft under-
belly and as they appeared from this difficult task, the lawnmower cut off the tip of
Cedric's tail!

- Chapter 12 -

It's the Knick-Knack Tree

The terrifying journey across Cedric's Field was finally over, but the dangers facing Willey and the Talking Teapot were not! The air was filled with the frantic buzzing of glow-bees and the last-ditch spluttering of the Gismo 500 lawnmower. The living bank of thorns was regrouping relentlessly and the lawnmower could not hold it back. The murky Mists of Time were closing in and the only light came from the fascinating dance of glow-bees disturbed from their nest.

"It's The Knick-Knack Tree!" whispered Willey. Its trunk was clearly visible and its bark was beginning to move.

"He's still alive!" Willey whispered. His instincts were telling him to be cautious and they were right. The deadly, venomous thorns were alive to every sound and movement and even as Willey watched, the thorns tightened their grip around the Knick-Knack Tree's trunk and outstretched branches.

"It's the Knick-Knack Tree!" whispered Willey. Its trunk was clearly visible and its bark was beginning to move.

And then, just at the moment when it appeared they might be safe, the thorns turned on them.

"The Sizing Stone, Willey – quick!"

The Talking Teapot's quick reactions were just in time. The thorns were closing in – they were all around them.

Willey could see the Knick-Knack Tree's dark, despairing eyes looking down at him, but there was nothing he could do, except try to escape and return to help another day.

Scrambling to their feet, the two intrepid runaways leapt on to a flat and well worn surface, just outside a hole in the Knick-Knack Tree's trunk. This was a magical Sizing Stone, the one the Fuddles had used when they first arrived here in Trickletown Valleys' Crater, and the moment their feet touched the top of it, they shrank to the size of the hole and dived straight in.

The tunnel inside the Knick-Knack Tree's roots was steep and winding and they didn't stop tumbling until they landed on a set of stone steps in front of a small wooden door.

"YIPP-EEEEE!" shouted the Talking Teapot, jumping joyfully to his feet, despite the alarming events of the past few minutes.

"HIGH FIVE, LOW FIVE, LAWN MOWER DRIVE – WE'RE STILL ALIVE!" shouted the Talking Teapot, dancing and jumping about in the dim and dusty hollow.

"Well you two took your time! I was expecting you here at least an hour ago."

The door to the Knick-Knack Tree's den had been opened.

"KNICKY-KNACKY!" shouted the Talking Teapot, leading the three of them off around the den, in a dance of cuddling delight. It was as if they had not seen one other since the disappearance of the Million Wiggle Fish Pond, which of course they had not.

Knicky-Knacky, the Knick-Knack Tree's closest and most cherished companion, lived in a den among the Knick-Knack Tree's roots and was exceptionally well suited for a life among the trees of the Emerald Forest.

And then, just at the moment when it appeared they might be safe, the thorns
turned on them.
"*The Sizing Stone, Willey – quick!*" shouted the Talking Teapot.

"SHUSH!" interrupted Knicky-Knacky. In the stillness, the buzzing of the glow-bees could be heard as they delivered honey to the lamps and wax to the candles – there was also a faint noise coming from somewere outside of the den!

"Whats that noise?" whispered Teabags. High in the Knick-Knack Tree's trunk they could hear the sound of scratching on the den's front door. In a flickety-tick, Knicky-Knacky was gone!

"Ta'wit-ta'whoo!" he shouted, disappearing up a set of spiralling steps, into the hollow of the trunk.

"It's Ta'wit-ta'whoo! It must be!"

He returned in no time at all, followed closely by a brown-feathered owl. To Willey it looked a little scary, as of course, thanks to the Sizing Stone, he was now a little smaller than the owl.

"Ta'wit-ta'whoo," said the owl, discarding the chewed remains of a sprig of thorns onto the open fire.

The thorns just hissed and spat as they crawled up the chimney.

"I bring you important information," hooted the owl, "but I cannot stop for long, as the thorns will soon be after me."

Ta'wit-ta'whoo lifted her wing and to Willey's complete surprise, there was the Orange Envelope hidden beneath it!

The envelope read out its letter. It knew exactly what was in it so didn't even bother to open it.

"I bring you important information," hooted the owl. Ta'wit-ta'whoo lifted her wing and to Willey's complete surprise, there was the Orange Envelope hidden beneath it!

"Willey

CONGRATULATIONS, you have reached the Knick-Knack Tree's den, but the path that lies ahead will not be easy.

The Hour-Glass Key has been stolen. It locks the Million Wiggle Fish Pond beneath The Gambit. And as you know, the seven Rainbow Fish are missing too; they are no longer hovering around the edge of the pool, controlling its waters. If the Hour Glass Key and the Rainbow Fish are not returned with the Emerald Ring, Trickletown's rivers will run dry and all the Million Wiggle Fish will perish.

You must find them and bring them back, before the end of the Trickletown Valleys' Games.

If you fail, the Mists of Time will take over Trickletown and the place where adventures begin and dreams come true may be lost for ever.

You must visit Old Man Moon and his Sack of Secrets. Here you will learn what has happened to the Rainbow Fish and who is using the Hour Glass Key and where to find it."

Teabags will help you on your journey and Knicky-Knacky will give you your final instructions.

So Good Luck
Q-O-F (The Queen of Fuddles)"

BANG! Everyone jumped as the door to the Knick-Knack Tree's den slammed shut.

"That was Ta'wit-ta'whoo, the Queen's Messenger," whispered Knicky-Knacky. The owl had vanished.

"That was the 'brown-feathered' bird who took my letter!" said Willey, remembering how one of his letters had been torn from his fingers.

"And the letters from Q-O-F: the Queen of Fuddles ... She was the lady in my dream! The one with the crown of gold and the jars of wiggly goldfish!" A curtain in a corner of the den began to shudder! The Million Wiggle Fish did not like being referred to as simply 'GOLD FISH'.

Willey was beginning to make sense of things ...

"Yes indeed you are right," said Knicky-Knacky, "and these are the Queen of Fuddle's Fish."

He drew back the curtain to reveal the seven glass jars Willey had talked about. Seven 'Million Wiggle Fish' were staring back at him.

"Now, let us see which one would like to come with you, and help you on your journey to find Old Man Moon and his Sack of Secrets."

Knicky-Knacky handed Willey a jar; the three of them waited ...

It was the tradition for Million Wiggle Fish to choose for themselves: they considered themselves far too important to be chosen by a Fuddle.

The Million Wiggle Fish blew bubbles, and then the Orange Fish jumped. It was followed very closely by the Blue, the Yellow, the Green and then the Red, until finally all the fish were swimming in Willey's jar.

"A full set of fish," chuckled Knicky-Knacky. "They must all be very keen to join in your adventure! But don't let them argue with each other, or you will not get the best out of any of them."

Knicky-Knacky placed a set of Million Wiggle Fish Instructions in Willey's hand and gave him important information for the rest of his journey.

He told Willey:

How to look after the Fish.

How to get out of Trickletown Valleys' Crater.

How to find Old Man Moon and his Sack of Secrets.

And how to avoid any traps set by the Mists of Time!

Willey and the Talking Teapot stood and listened ...

The water in the jars began to bubble, and then the Orange Fish jumped. It was followed very closely by the Blue, the Yellow, the Green and then the Red, until finally all the Million Wiggle Fish were swimming round in Willey's jar.

The clock on top of the book case started to chime. It was nine o'clock already and in only one hour's time, the Trickletown Valleys' Games were due to begin.

"Quick!" said Knicky-Knacky, opening one of many doors to let them out.

"There is no more time to waste. Follow the passage to the left until you reach the Emerald Lake."

"Be careful, Willey, and good luck," were the last words either of them heard, as the door slammed shut behind them.

This was a different tunnel – it was covered in tentacles. Spindly, green, thin ones, and they were wriggling around in the darkness, trying to find out who was in there.

"Follow me," said Teabags, grabbing hold of the jar of Wiggle Fish and shaking it up a bit. "Million Wiggle Fish glow in the dark, if you make them angry."

The Talking Teapot was right, but it wasn't the best thing to do when you needed their help!

It took Teabags all of their time in the tunnel to calm them down again.

This was a different tunnel — it was covered in tentacles. Spindly, green, thin ones, and they were wriggling around in the darkness, trying to find out who was in there.

121

They reached a wall of water.

"This is the underground Emerald Lake," said Teabags. "And I hope you don't mind getting wet because this is our only way out."

Willey looked worried, as he wasn't quite sure how he was going to breathe under water, and there were many fishy faces staring back at him – not all of them friendly.

The journey through the Emerald Lake was certainly not easy. Willey had to turn the Talking Teapot upside down and stretch it over his own head so he could breathe – like the mask of a deep sea diver, but without any windows. The only problem was that he could not see where he was going, so it was up to the Talking Teapot to give directions.

"Three steps forward and a step to the left," said Teabags. It should have been a step to the right, but it was not that easy to give the correct instructions when you were upside-down! Willey was swept off his feet and if it hadn't been for the Million Wiggle Fish this might well have been the end of our story.

They guided Willey and the Talking Teapot around whirlpools and rocks. They had a fight with a cuttlefish and a shark. Then finally, after almost being eaten by an eel, they brought Willey and the Talking Teapot back to Trickletown, through the rim of an empty 'This & That' pipe.

Willey and the Talking Teapot and the jar of Million Wiggle Fish emerged from the pipe to see a large crowd gathering around Inner Street. The Trickletown Valleys' Games were soon to begin!

They reached a wall of water.
This is the underground Emerald Lake," said Teabags. "And I hope you don't
mind getting wet, because this is our only way out."

- Chapter 13 -

The Trickletown Valleys' Games

Tacticus Meticulous was looking for his whistle!

"Bother me britches!" muttered Tacticus. "What in the name of Trickletown has happened to my–"

CRASH! Another drawer full of 'This & That' spilled over the dining-room table.

"–WHISTLE!" shouted Tacticus, rummaging around amongst an ever increasing mountain of 'This & That' which he knew did not contain his whistle – but he didn't know where else to look for it.

"Bother me … bother me … bother …"

Soon there were no more drawers to be emptied, but still the bothersome whistle was nowhere to be found.

"Whatever are you up to, Tacticus? And may I suggest you take a look at your watch? If you are not very careful you will be late!"

Mrs Meticulous was rather concerned, but Tacticus *(who you may remember as the Ring Master from the Trickletown Valleys' Circus)* was well aware of the time – this was the reason he was searching for his whistle.

"And if you are looking for your whistle I have put it on top of your lunch box," added Mrs Meticulous.

PSSST – another of Mr and Mrs What'Notts' 'memory-loss', air fresheners squirted him, full in the face! The spray appeared to be working, as Tacticus was forgeting where he had put things! Tacticus growled, and after pausing for a moment to compose himself, raced back into the kitchen, grabbed hold of his lunch box and his whistle, and without saying a single word to his wife, darted out of the house, like a mouse out of a cheese box, in the direction of Orange Street Stadium.

To begin with Orange Street was empty. There was hardly a sound to be heard, except for the whistling of the breeze around Tacticus' large floppy ears and the rippling of the coat tails on his fine black moleskin suit, trimmed with gold.

"TACTICUS IS COMING ..." "HERE COMES TACTICUS ..." "MAKE WAY FOR TACTICUS ..."

Tacticus could hear the chanting of the crowds. They had gathered to watch the spectacular opening to the Trickletown Valleys' Games. However, the games could not begin until Tacticus blew his whistle.

Tacticus was never usually late for anything. "Tacticus is meticulous," his friends always said, but this morning things were different.

His memory was beginning to fade, thanks to Mr and Mrs What'Notts' mysterious air freshener. From the moment he got out of bed, things had gone wrong.

To begin with, his alarm clock didn't go off. Then he went to put on his clothes, but he had forgotten where they were. He had forgotten to polish his shoes and he forgot to finish his breakfast. And as for his bothersome whistle! We can only guess at what had happened to that, before it finally found its place on top of his lunch box.

However, all that really mattered at that moment was that Tacticus was late, and that the Indigo Street Church Clock was striking ten o'clock.

Tacticus placed his whistle between his lips as he entered Orange Street Stadium.

"Get a move on Tacticus!" shouted the Mayor. "And you had better make it snappy!"

The Mayor was laughing and so was everyone else, because a pair of crocodile slippers were busily snapping at Tacticus's toes.

There was no more time to waste. So, taking the longest, deepest breath he had ever taken, on the strike of ten o'clock, TACTICUS BLEW HIS WHISTLE ...

"Block up the pipes!" shouted the Mayor. "Block up the pipes!"

The crowds chanted his command and the giant coconut corks were plunged into the tops of the 'This & That' pipes. The Labyrinth's exits were sealed and the pressures beneath the ground began to build. It was not very long before the earth at the centre of The Gambit started to move.

There was no more time to waste. So, taking the longest, deepest breath he had ever taken, on the strike of ten o'clock, *TACTICUS BLEW HIS WHISTLE ...*

Seven circular platforms rose one after the other, each one larger than the one before, until the centre of The Gambit resembled an enormous wedding cake. It looked almost as high as the mountains, and from the sluices on the top of its walls, the seven Trickletown Rivers cascaded over its edge.

B O O M! Indigo Basin erupted. The Trickletown Valleys' Games had begun and teams from each coloured street began to race to the top of the 'Wedding Cake'.

Tacticus collapsed on the steps of Orange Street Stadium. He was completely 'whistled out' and, to add to his embarrassment, his favourite crocodile slippers had lost all their teeth.

"Glad you could make it Tacticus," chuckled the Mayor.

"Give me an 'I'"   "I"

"Give me an 'N'"   "N"

"Give me a 'D'"   "D"

"Give me an 'I'"   "I"

"Give me a 'G'"   "G"

"Give me an 'O'"   "O"

"AND WHAT HAVE YOU GOT?"

" I N D I G O "

Deafening cheers rang out around Indigo Street – their team was first to the top. Indigo Street always won the Trickletown Valleys' Games' Grand Trophy and they always won the race to the top of the 'Wedding Cake'. Their three-man team was the Balancing Cubonyento Brothers from the magnificent Trickletown Valleys' Circus and nobody could beat them.

Seven circular platforms rose one after the other, each one larger than the one before, until the centre of The Gambit resembled an enormous wedding cake.

"Indigo Street twelve points," instructed the Mayor, as the Cubonyento Brothers hoisted their victory flag on the pole at the top of the 'Wedding Cake'.

"Yellow Street: ten points."

"Green Street: eight points."

"Orange Street: six points."

"Blue Street: four points."

"Red Street: two points."

"Violet Street: one point."

Following the completion of this spectacular opening challenge, the 'Wedding Cake' lowered itself to the ground. The next of the Seven Trickletown challenges was now ready to begin – 'The race over Trickletown Gambit' – but things at the centre of Trickletown were never quite as simple as they might first appear!

Willey and the Talking Teapot and the jar of Million Wiggle Fish watched and waited, as the different challenges came and went. The scores were beginning to build up and the crowds were getting more and more excited.

It was time to put their secret plan into action! So taking the jar of fish with him, Teabags disappeared from the scene.

Other things were happening too!

The mysterious Mists of Time were making their move – this was their chance to take over Trickletown. They were controlling the *fading* figures of Mr Got-a-Lott and Mr and Mrs What'Nott, who were looking rather pleased. They were sure they had locked Willey up in his bedroom the previous night, and with Willey out of the way, soon the secrets of Trickletown (so they thought) might all be theirs! They could destroy what was left of the Knick-Knack Tree and – thanks to the 'memory-loss' spray – none of the Fuddles would remember anything about it.

"Chaseboard Challenge get set!" shouted the Mayor.

The final challenge of the Games was about to begin and the tips of all the Chaseboards lit to amber.

At precisely this moment, Willey steered his Chaseboard into Orange Street Stadium, to a cheer from the Orange Street crowd. Mr and Mrs What'Nott almost fell off their seats. Mr Got-a-Lott actually did, and his false moustache stuck to his chin.

BEEP!

"Nice of you to join us, Willey," sneered his fiercest Chaseboard Challenger, Zack Cubonyento. "I was beginning to think you had given up on this challenge – you have no chance of winning the Grand Trophy for Orange Street. I'm going to make sure of that!"

BEEP!

Zack was probably right, but Willey didn't even bother to look at him, he had much more important things to worry about.

BEEP!

The final challenge of the Games had now begun!

The crowds around Trickletown cheered as the challengers sped out of Orange Street Stadium and clattered through the chaos of In-a-Pickle Farmyard. The hens dived straight for the hen house as the racers jumped the water trough.

Milk Shake and Crunch spat out the cuds they were chewing for the second time that day, hitting the hollow tin walls of Big Bale Barn, 'BOOM BOOM', one after the other.

Farmer Crisp, still recovering from his flight through the bedroom window, let out an angry roar from the seat of his wheelchair. The challengers raced on.

Setting the pace at the front of the Chaseboard Challenge was Ruby Taught'It, from Red Street. Her dad was the school headmaster and she was the best Chaseboard challenger in Trickletown. She was heading for Red Ned's Rapids, and for those who were brave enough to follow, they were in for a very rough ride.

"Rapid sensors on!" instructed Willey, as his Chaseboard hit the water. He immediately swerved to avoid a row of shivering rocks. Zack Cubonyento smiled as he zoomed straight past him.

The Challenge was not going well for Willey, but at least he was still in the race. Finally when he did catch up, it was time to put his secret plan into action!

"Sonic Thrust!" commanded Willey, and he immediately shot to the front. Now all the Chaseboard Challengers would have to follow him.

Willey's Chaseboard glided in and out the trees through the Dangling Forest and took the race onto Awesome Plateau; here they would need to be careful to avoid any traps set by the Mists of Time. Then suddenly the race took a dive over Dangerous Ridge and Willey zoomed into the entrance of Orange Street Mine. The glow of the Chaseboard tip lights was all that shone in the darkness ... until Orange Street Labyrinth turned all its lights on.

Willey fumbled around in his pocket for the map which Teabags had given him:

'Turn right, to avoid the entrance to Trickletown's Labyrinths.
Left and immediately down, before the Sticky Rocks grab you.
Take your chance through the Cavern of Tricks.
Right, left and right around the Cauldron of Indigo Basin and then up until you reach the all-seeing eye of Blue Street Labyrinth.'

"Rapid sensors on!" instructed Willey, as his Chaseboard hit the water. He immediately swerved to avoid a row of shivering rocks. Zack Cubonyento smiled as he zoomed straight past him.

W O O O S H! Willey burst out back into the sunlight. He was still leading the race, but the energy and the speed of his Chaseboard had virtually gone.

There was no time to waste. Willey placed the Golden Ring of his Time-Line carefully on the tip of his Chaseboard. Then taking one giant leap into the air, he left most of the inhabitants of Trickletown, his Chaseboard and his fellow Chaseboard Challengers suspended in time.

When he landed back on the ground, everything behind him looked still.

A rainbow of light burst out from the silver ring of his Time-Line. It would lead Willey safely back to the Trickletown and the Golden Ring of his Time-Line when he was ready to return.

But what Willey failed to notice, was the appearance of four more rainbows.

Willey was being followed, but by who?

"High Five, low five, the Chaseboard Challenge is still alive!" shouted Teabags excitedly, appearing from behind some bushes. He had masterminded their escape. "Congratulations Willey! You are leading the Chaseboard Challenge, and now Trickletown is frozen in time, there is nothing anyone else can do about it! Well, at least not until we return."

Teabags had been unaffected by the freezing of time, thanks to the collective powers of their new companions – the jar of Mllion Wiggle Fish.

Willey and the Talking Teapot laughed together. For them, the plan, had worked perfectly. Everyone would have to wait to see who would win the Chaseboard Challenge and the Trickletown Valleys' Games' Grand Trophy.

Willey placed the Golden Ring of his Time-Line carefully on the tip of his Chaseboard. Then taking one giant leap into the air, he left most of the inhabitants of Trickletown, his Chaseboard and his fellow Chaseboard Challengers suspended in time.

- Chapter 14 -

A Journey to Remember

Willey's departure from the Chaseboard Challenge had left him approaching Blue Street Station, but this was no ordinary station!

This was a station to the stars.

Blue Street Space Station had been built near the top of Blue Street to allow the Fuddles to travel into space. It was one of Willey's favourite places and one day he hoped to have a space pod all of his own.

"You must visit Old Man Moon and his Sack of Secrets," the Orange Envelope had said.

Well this was exactly where they were going – and the space pod sitting on the launch pad was waiting to take them there.

"Jump aboard, Willey!" shouted Teabags, his finger hovering over a large green button. "Strap yourself in and I will get this thing ready for take-off."

Teabags looked at all the instruments flickering in front of him. The Wiggle Fish Control Globe was activated. And there was nothing telling him they should not take off, so when they were both good and ready, he pressed the large green button.

"Jump aboard, Willey!" shouted Teabags, his finger hovering over a large green button. "Strap yourself in and I will get this thing ready for take-off."

"Old Man Moon here we come!" declared Teabags, releasing a head of steam from the end of his spout. His lid was beginning to rattle.

"Have you ever flown one of these before?" enquired Willey, as the space pod zoomed into orbit.

Teabags did not reply – he was too busy fiddling with the controls.

After two near misses with a satellite and a brush with a bright shooting star, Willey concluded that Teabags hadn't. So he took hold of the controls himself, and just in time! The troublesome Comet, called Climaticus, whizzed past the cockpit, sending the space pod spinning off in a different direction.

"WARNING! WARNING! WARNING!" A red light flashed across the centre of the control panel. "UNAUTHORISED SPACE PODS APPROACHING."

Willey looked at the radar indicator and sure enough there were three more space pods following close behind.

"WARP DRIVE: EMERGENCY SYSTEMS ACTIVATED," announced the control panel. Willey just followed the on-screen instructions as the space pod took evasive action. However, there was nothing anyone could do. Someone had programmed the space pods to follow each other on their missions, so wherever the leading pod went the others could only follow.

"IMMINENT COLLISION!
PREPARE FOR EMERGENCY LANDING!"
S N A P !   T W A N G !   C R A C K !

Willey took hold of the controls for himself, and just in time, as the troublesome Comet, called Climaticus, whizzed past the cockpit.

The space pod tangled itself in Old Man Moon's beard and it was followed very swiftly by a *Whiz, a Whoosh and a Swoosh* as the three other space pods followed in close pursuit.

"FIRE IN THE ENGINES!" shouted Teabags, and sure enough a bright orange glow could be seen outside the window.

"OLD MAN MOON IS ON FIRE! ACTIVATE THE EXTINGUISHERS!" but it was far too late for that, the flames had set light to his beard and the smoke was drifting up his nose.

"Ah ... Ahhh ... Ahhhh ... C H O O O ...!

Old Man Moon sneezed, and the space pods shot like rockets out of his beard. Even the Comet Climaticus was thrown out of orbit. As the space pods hurtled through space, they were heading for the one thing that might stop them. A small orange planet – Planet Fuddle.

"RE-CALCULATING CURRENT DESTINATION," said the control panel, as they skimmed the icy waves of an Orange Ocean and then ploughed into the frosty trees of a Flooded Forest.

It had not been the most comfortable of rides, but eventually they came to a stop.

"JOURNEY TIME: FOURTEEN MINUTES – DISTANCE TRAVELLED: TEN MILLION WIGGLES – LOCATION: PLANET FUDDLE," concluded the control panel, before lowering the revs of the engine and switching off.

It had been less than twenty minutes since Willey left the Chaseboard Challenge, yet now he was floating in a space pod, in the middle of a slushy orange lake, on a strange, but not so distant planet called Fuddle. And what's more, he could see a large wooden galleon heading straight for them!

As the space pods hurtled through space, they were heading for the one thing that might stop them. A small orange planet – Planet Fuddle.

Ding-Ding! Ding-Ding! Ding-Ding!

Alarm bells started to ring in the Flooded Forest; HMS *Rattle* was afloat and her captain was sounding the alarm.

"All hands on deck! Hoist the mainsail! Anchors aweigh!"

The bow wave swept the pods aside as the ship sailed past and then drifted back into the mist as curiously and swiftly as it had arrived.

It was Willey who first broke the silence. "I wonder what happened to the others," he said, fiddling with the buttons on the radar, but the signal was no longer working.

Teabags tried the radio: "Calling all space pods ... Calling all space pods. Is anyone out there, receiving me? Over."

Willey and Teabags waited, but there was no reply.

Teabags tried again: "Attention all space pods, is anyone in need of assistance? Over."

The radio crackled and then came a response that neither of them expected: "Hearing you loud and clear. Yeah, we're cool out here, but where in the heavens did all those space pods happen to come from? Over."

This was not a voice that either of them recognised, so Teabags called again:

"Please identify yourself and confirm your current position. Over."

Teabags waited for an answer ...

Alarm bells started to ring in the Flooded Forest; HMS Rattle was afloat and her captain was sounding the alarm.

"Hi, this is Dude, dude, and we are the Pie-Rat Gang from the Sleeping Planet. You have just released our galleon from the Flooded Forest and we are anchored off the rocks in Biscuit Bay. Over."

"The Pie-Rats!" said Teabags, quickly turning off the radio. "The notorious Pie-Rat Gang from the Sleeping Planet!" Knicky-Knacky had told him many stories about them and none were good!

There was a very loud knock on the space pod door.

Willey and the Talking Teapot froze to the spot. If this was the Pie-Rat Gang, they were both in trouble. The knock on the door came again, but this time it was followed by a voice that Willey knew.

"Let me in, Willey! Quick! The trees are chasing me!"

The knocking got even louder, before Willey managed to open the door. It was Eddy, Willey's best friend. He was petrified, freezing and fortunately on his own.

"How on earth did you manage to follow us? And who is in the other two space pods?" Willey asked. Because if Eddy had managed to follow them, there could be literally *anyone from Trickletown* hiding out there!

"A Time-Line," replied Eddy. "That is how I managed to follow you. I grabbed a hand full from the box in the A to Z Alley, as I escaped from Mr Got-a-Lott in the Got-a-Lott Museum.

"Then when everyone was watching the Trickletown Valleys' Games the next morning, I crept into Blue Street Town Hall and watched to see where you were heading on the Trickletown Time Model.

"The Talking Teapot was at blue Street Station, so I guessed you might be heading towards the space pods.

"As to who else might have followed us! I have no idea! Other than I did have the feeling someone was watching me, from among the shadows, in Blue Street Town Hall."

"The Pie-Rats!" said Teabags, quickly turning off the radio. "The notorious Pie-Rat Gang from the Sleeping Planet!" Knicky-Knacky had told him many stories about them and none were good!

It was strange to think that only a short while ago, Willey had gazed up at the Moon from his bedroom window and seen the two distinctive eyes peering back at him.

He had travelled through Time; beneath a circus tent; to a place where "Adventures Begin and Dreams Come True" – but everything seemed to have gone wrong. The magical Million Wiggle Fish Pond had been locked beneath the surface of Trickletown. The magnificent Knick-Knack Tree was being held prisoner by the Mists of Time, and the Fuddles were all losing their memories thanks to Willey's mum and dad and their mysterious 'memory-loss' spray.

Willey had been sent on an adventure to find the Hour Glass Key and the Rainbow Fish, but his journey to Old Man Moon had been a disaster. Now the night was drawing in and he was floating in a space pod among the terrifying trees in a Flooded Forest, on a small orange planet called Fuddle – and between him and the rest of his adventure stood the notorious Pie-Rat Gang and their galleon – HMS *Rattle*.

"Well that was a journey to remember," said Teabags, breathing a sigh of relief.

Unfortunatly neither Teabags nor Willey had noticed the dangerous trees approaching their space pod.

Willey had been sent on an adventure to find the Hour Glass Key and the Rainbow Fish, but his journey to Old Man Moon had been a disaster. Now he was floating in a space pod among the terrifying trees in a Flooded Forest, on a small orange planet called Fuddle.

- Chapter 15 -

Escape from HMS *Rattle*

Rooter, Captain of the Pie-Rat Gang, was fast asleep in his cabin. The sun was beginning to rise over the Moving Mountains and his galleon, HMS *Rattle,* was anchored off the rocks in Biscuit Bay.

"COCK-A-DOODLY-DOO," could be heard from the top of the crow's nest.

Rooter woke up with a start. He had never heard such a noise first thing in the morning. But this was only the start of it.

"WAKEY-WAKEY RISE AND SHINE, IT'S TIME TO GET UP IT'S HALF PAST NINE!" shouted Brown Bottom at the top of his voice.

It was really only six o'clock, but he wanted to make sure that everyone got up. He could see a space pod floating towards them and it was being *chased by the Flooded Forest!*

Ding-Ding! Ding-Ding! Ding-Ding!

Alarm bells were ringing again on HMS *Rattle,* but this time, it was Fetch, farmer Crisp's faithful bloodhound, who was sounding the alarm!

He and Brown Bottom had found two of Eddy's discarded Time-Lines; this allowed them to escape the Trickletown Valleys' Games; now still frozen in time.

Following the Talking Teapot to Blue Street Station, they jumped aboard an empty space pod, because now they know the Talking Teapot's magic water allows them to speak; their plan is to follow the Teapot where ever it goes.

Scared by the terrifying trees in the Flooded Forest, Brown Bottom and Fetch took their chance to escape their gripping branches, and swam towards the Pie-Rats' galleon during the night. They climbed the anchor chain to the main deck, where they hid among some barrels and baskets.

Rooter's cabin door burst open. "CATCH THAT CONFOUNDED COCKEREL! I WANT COCKEREL PIE FOR MY BREAKFAST!" commanded Rooter.

But at that moment, everyone saw the Flooded Forest, and a space pod, heading towards the ship!

And once you get caught by the Flooded Forest, it is very difficult to escape!

"ALL HANDS ON DECK! HOIST THE MAINSAIL! ANCHORS AWEIGH!" shouted Rooter.

As HMS *Rattle* headed for the open water, Fetch and Brown Bottom were forgotten about in the commotion.

Willey, Eddy, Teabags and the jar of Million Wiggle Fish were still struggling to catch up in their space pod. They had decided their chances were better on the Pie-Rats' galleon than trapped among the terrifying trees in the Flooded Forest. Eventually, they were roped to the stern of the galleon by the excited Pie-Rats – then the space pod, the galleon and everyone on it made their escape.

"CATCH ME THAT COCKEREL. FETCH ME THAT HOUND AND BRING ME WHOEVER IS TRAVELLING ABOARD THAT SPACE POD!" Rooter shouted his commands as the Pie-Rats scampered about the ship.

But when they looked the space pod was empty – the inhabitants had secretly crept aboard HMS *Rattle* – and the Pie-Rats returned empty-handed.

Rooter sniffed at the air. His whiskers were starting to twitch. He knew there were Fuddles somewhere aboard his ship and it would only be a matter of time before he caught them.

"Set all the traps and warm up the ovens," instructed Rooter. "We are going to eat Fuddle pie tonight."

He scurried back to his cabin to check his treasure.

It was not very long before the ship was covered in traps. The Pie-Rats hid in the shadows, watching and waiting ...

The Pie-Rats originally came from the Sleeping Planet. They had mastered the art of space flight, and used their wooden galleon as a space craft to travel from one mysterious planet to another. As their name suggests they loved to eat pies, and scoured the surrounding universe for new ingredients to make them. They had been trapped in the Flooded Forest for quite some time, before the space pods crash landed and released them and were all very keen to try some more pie recipes.

"It appears to have all gone quiet," whispered Willey, creeping out of the cupboard where they were hiding. Teabags shook up the jar of Wiggle Fish, which lit up the room.

The walls were covered with shelves, and the shelves were laden with pies: Fish Pies, Granny Pies, Monster Pies, Pig's Ear Pies, Empty Pies ...

"Fuddle Pies!" gasped Eddy.

What made matters worse was that this shelf was empty! And there was a note on the shelf which said: *Rooter's favourite – tell the Cook to bake more pies'*.

"We have got to get off this ship," whispered Willey," moving faster and nearer to the door. Then ... CLUNK! CRACK! WHIP! SNAP!

They were trapped under a large woven basket, and Pie-Rat traps went off all over the ship.

"LAY OUT THE TABLES. ROLL OUT THE PASTRY!" shouted Rooter, licking his lips. "WE ARE GOING TO HAVE FUDDLE PIE TONIGHT."

It was true. They had all been captured. Willey and Eddy, Brown Bottom, Fetch, Teabags and the jar of Million Wiggle Fish were locked in a cage in the cook house to await their fate.

But someone else was already hiding in the cook house. He had followed them here in one of the space pods and sneaked aboard the Pie-Rats' galleon during the night!

Teabags shook up the jar of Wiggle Fish, which lit up the room.
The walls were covered with shelves, and the shelves were laden with pies.

A figure appeared from among the shadows, dressed as a cook. "Welcome," said the Cook. "Welcome to the end of your adventure!"

The Cook (whoever he was) chuckled. There was something very familiar about his voice and Willey noticed he was wearing a false moustache!

"It's the large round Ticket Collector, Mr Got-a-Lott!" gasped Willey. You could virtually see straight through him.

"Yes," replied Mr Got-a-Lott, curling one end of his moustache between his fingers. "Your plan to freeze everyone in time during the Trickletown Valleys' Games did not work, as I was wearing a Time-Line."

Willey looked at the silver ring on Mr Got-a-Lott's finger.

"After allowing Eddy to escape from the Got-a-lott Museum, he stole some Time-Lines. So I then kept a close eye on him. During the Trickletown Valleys' Games I followed him into Blue Street Town Hall to the Trickletown Time Model. He should have realised I might have been following him, and was hiding among the shadows. We both watched you and the Talking Teapot moving on the model. I knew you would all meet up at some time or other."

Mr Got-a-Lott sharpened his knife as he prepared to follow the Pie-Rats' secret recipe for Fuddle Pie.

Fetch growled and Willey suddenly felt very nervous ...

However, help was on hand.

"Ta'wit-ta'whoo," said an owl, as she dropped the Orange Envelope into the cook house.

Mr Got-a-Lott was too busy chopping up herbs to notice that anything had happened.

Using some trickery, the Orange Envelope unlocked the door of the cage before slipping inside. It had a message of its own that it wanted to deliver: *"Old Man Moon is almost overhead,"* whispered the envelope, *"and he is gathering up everyone's secrets. You must climb the forward mast and write your secrets on the sails. But look out for Good Old Henry – the captain's ginger cat! If he sees those Million Wiggle Fish, he will make short work of them."*

Mr Got-a-Lott sharpened his knife as he prepared to follow the Pie-Rats' secret recipe for Fuddle Pie.

Before any questions could be asked, the wind blew the Orange Envelope straight out of the window, and fortunately for Willey and Eddy, it was followed by the Pie-Rats' secret recipe for Fuddle Pie.

With the door of the cage now open, the stowaways crept out of the cook house ...

Nobody was on the main deck.

The Pie-Rat gang were gathered up on the poop deck counting treasure and Good Old Henry, the captain's cat, was nowhere to be seen. Only his empty red-hot Million Wiggle Fish dish sat by the door of the cook house.

One by one they tiptoed over the decks and climbed the forward mast. Then one by one they began to write secrets on the sail.

When I go to bed at night I keep a picture of my pet dog Badsey under my pillow, wrote Willey.

The wind blew softly on the sails, and the ship moved forward ...

I always warm my pot before I make a pot of tea, wrote Teabags.

The sails of HMS *Rattle* stiffened out and the ship gained speed ...

My dad has great big holes in all his socks, wrote Eddy and everyone chuckled.

It was then that they began to realise what was happening: Old Man Moon's large paddle was creating a wind and the wind was gathering up the secrets they were writing on the sail.

"Quick!" said Willey, looking at Brown Bottom and Fetch. "Write one of your secrets on the sail, it will give us more speed."

I occasionally sit on an egg when the hens aren't looking, pecked Brown Bottom.

Farmer Crisp has a picture of a bear tattooed on his BU– but before he could finish the word *'BUM',* the ship took off, leaving the seas of Planet Fuddle far below. They were heading for Old Man Moon, and there was nothing the Pie-Rat gang or Mr Got-a-Lott could do to stop them.

One by one they tiptoed over the decks and climbed the forward mast. Then one by one they began to write secrets on the sail.

The cook house door flew open.

"CATCH THOSE CONFOUNDED FUDDLES – THEY HAVE ALL ESCAPED!" bellowed Mr Got-a-Lott.

Rooter was certainly surprised to see Mr Got-a-Lott running out of his kitchen, but he quickly sounded the alarm:

Ding-Ding! Ding-Ding! Ding-Ding!

"A handful of treasure for anyone who catches those Fuddles!" instructed Rooter. "And where is Good Old Henry? Send him after those Million Wiggle Fish; he can eat 'em for his dinner."

But Rooter needn't have worried; Good Old Henry had smelt the fish and was already halfway up the forward mast – he liked nothing better than a dish full of tasty Million Wiggle Fish.

There was chaos aboard HMS *Rattle* as the Pie-Rats scoured the decks – and one by one got caught in their very own traps.

"Land ahoy!" shouted Brown Bottom. They had almost made it back to Old Man Moon.

"CATCH THOSE CONFOUNDED FUDDLES – THEY HAVE ALL ESCAPED!" bellowed Mr Got-a-Lott.
Rooter was certainly surprised to see Mr Got-a-Lott running out of his kitchen, but he quickly sounded the alarm.

157

HMS *Rattle* creaked and groaned as the wind blew hard on its sails.

"When I give you the command to jump, grab hold of the sail!" shouted Teabags. "We will parachute down into Old Man Moon's Sack of Secrets."

A large grey shadow of a cat crept over them. They had no idea of the danger heading their way.

"POUNCE!" shouted Rooter.

"JUMP!" shouted Teabags, cutting loose the sail.

"TA'WIT-TA'WHOO!" screeched an owl, and they jumped.

Every one of them – Willey, Eddy, Brown Bottom, Fetch and the Talking Teapot sailed away – Good Old Henry stole the Wiggle Fish Jar, and Ta'wit-ta'whoo, now keeping a distant, but watchfull eye on our Knick-Knack Tree Adventurers, glided safely on the wind.

Good Old Henry headed straight for his red-hot Million Wiggle Fish dish, which was scorching in the heat of the sun.

"Good Old Henry," said Rooter, removing the lid from the jar and pouring its contents into the dish. Good Old Henry purred as the water steamed and sizzled, and licked his lips in anticipation of a large tasty dish of Wiggle Fish! But when all the steam had disappeared, the Fish Dish was empty – somehow every one had escaped! Rooter was not happy at all.

Good Old Henry purred as the water steamed and sizzled, and licked his lips in anticipation of a large tasty dish of Million Wiggle Fish! But when all the steam had disappeared, the Million Wiggle Fish Dish was empty.

159

- Chapter 16 -

The Sack of Secrets

"Listen to this one," chuckled Willey. "Trim the Gardner says that rubbing soap on all the leaves keeps the rabbits off his cucumbers."

Everyone laughed.

"And here's another," said Eddy, plucking another secret out of the air, as the friends drifted endlessly down into the seemingly bottomless Sack of Secrets.

"Rooter sucks his thumb when he's sitting on the toilet."

Everyone laughed so much they almost let go of the sail they were holding on to.

"Mr Got-a-Lott picks his nose at the bottom of the garden."

"Trim the Gardener is secretly in love with Mrs Merry'Feathers."

"Mrs Merry'Feathers can't stop laughing when she tickles her own feet."

"Ivor Sack'Full holds his letters up to the light to see what's in them."

"The Mayor of Trickletown's favourite sweets are gooseberry toffees."

Thump! Finally they had reached the bottom of Old Man Moon's Sack of Secrets.

Everyone laughed.
"And here's another," said Eddy, plucking another secret out of the air, as the
friends drifted endlessly down into the seemingly bottomless
Sack of Secrets.

161

"Secrets to be kept to the left – secrets to be broken to the right – take the funny ones straight down the middle and give them to Dudley," said a small brown elf, carrying a large pile of secrets. "And you had better be quick before any of the secrets get out."

The elf disappeared into the distance, leaving Willey and his intrepid band of travellers to unravel themselves from the sail.

"Cock-a-Doodly-Doo," said Brown Bottom, who was in need of another drink of the Talking Teapot's water.

There appeared to be nothing else to do but follow the elf's instructions; which they did. They each gathered up a large pile of secrets from the floor of the sack and followed the elf's tiny footprints ...

The way ahead was lit by a beam of sunlight, shining in through a hole in the side of the sack. The floor was littered with paper.

They were passed by several more brown elves along the way and each one said the same thing:

"Secrets to be kept to the left – secrets to be broken to the right – take the funny ones straight down the middle and give them to Dudley. And you had better be quick before any of the secrets get out."

Willey was now very keen to meet Dudley, whoever he was. He was sure Dudley would be able to tell them where the Hour Glass Key had been taken and what had happened to the missing Rainbow Fish.

There appeared to be nothing else to do, but follow the elf's instructions; which they did. They each gathered up a large pile of secrets from the floor of the sack and followed the elf's tiny footprints ...

Gradually the beam of sunlight led them to Dudley: an extremely large and overweight hamster. He had become so big that his feet no longer touched the ground and the only way he could move was to wriggle.

Dudley was the Keeper of Secrets. He had been at the bottom of the sack for longer than anyone could remember, but his job was a very important one; in fact there were two very important jobs he was here to do.

First, as Keeper of Secrets, he would read each one – and then to make sure none of the secrets got out, he would try to eat them all. This was why he had become so fat. However, Dudley had a very good memory, so if you needed to know a certain secret, you should first make friends with Dudley.

Besides being Keeper of Secrets, Dudley was in charge of the Tablet of Light, the most important rock in the universe, for the Tablet of Light could see everything!

"Welcome," said Dudley, pausing to nibble his way through another pile of secrets. "So you need to know what happened to the Seven Rainbow Fish and the missing Hour Glass Key?"

Dudley already knew why everyone was here. The Orange Envelope had told him, even though Dudley had tried his best to eat it.

Dudley wriggled to one side to reveal the large grey rock he had been sitting on. "This is the Tablet of Light," said Dudley. "It will show us everything you need to know."

As the beam of sunlight lit the rock, the Tablet of Light changed colour and shape. Then, a moving picture appeared of what had *really* happened in Trickletown, on the night the Million Wiggle Fish Pond disappeared and the Fuddles began losing their memories.

"The Trouble in Trickletown began when a troublesome comet called Climaticus was circling the Earth," said Dudley. He then continued to explain the story the pictures were showing them.

Dudley wriggled to one side to reveal the large grey rock he had been sitting on.
"This is the Tablet of Light," said Dudley.
"It will show us everything you need to know."

"The winds around the centre of Trickletown had become extremely dangerous and Mr What'Nott needed help to secure the Million Wiggle Fish Pond beneath The Gambit.

"Mrs What'Nott, Willey and Mr Got-a-Lott had duly arrived to help – but to keep themselves safe in the Mists of Time, they had each made an extra copy of themselves. This was of course what all Fuddles do in times of danger. One of each of them remained in Key Stone Cottage, where they thought it was safe."

Dudley paused to nibble on yet another pile of secrets, and then keeping silent, he allowed The Tablet of Light continue to display its pictures:

Mr What'Nott, Willey and Mr Got-a-Lott arrived to help – but to keep themselves safe in the Mists of Time, they each made an extra body; now there were two identical versions of each of them.

Moving hand in hand, Mr and Mrs What'Nott, Willey and Mr Got-a-Lott walked to the Granite Key Stone. The wind was blowing hard and The Mists of Time were swirling around their ankles.

Then, linking arms, the other versions of Mr and Mrs What'Nott, Willey and Mr Got-a-Lott walked to the Granite Key Stone.

Mr What'Nott placed the Hour Glass Key in the Key Stone. He was about to lock it in with the Emerald Ring when the second Mr Got-a-Lott *(who had somehow been affected by the mist)* ran out from Key Stone Cottage. He stole the Hour Glass Key and released the Rainbow Fish – who guarded the Fish Pond – before running away with them all into the Mists of Time.

The Rainbow Fish followed Mr Got-a-Lott and the Hour Glass Key into the Mists of Time, and they all disappeared.

The Emerald Ring fell to the ground – and as the Fish Pond disappeared beneath The Gambit, *a mysterious hand reached out and grabbed the Emerald Ring.*

The picture on the Tablet of Light became covered in mist and when eventually everything cleared, the Fish Pond was gone, and for the What'Nott family who had remained in Key Stone Cottage, so, it appeared, had Trickletown. They were trapped in the Mists of Time, at the place where our story began. All that remained with the What'Notts was Key Stone Cottage, the seven large oak trees, a small insignificant stream and the fallen granite Key Stone.

Dudley had now finished nibbling on his pile of secrets and spoke again.

"Your *nasty* mum and dad and Mr Got-a-Lott are fast disappearing. The Mists of Time are taking over their bodies and are forcing them to help take over Trickletown. They have been given a misterious 'memory-loss' spray to help them do it, and it is making all the Fuddles lose their memories."

Your mum and dad have been selling them in their corner shop, and now these dangerious sprays can be found all over Trickletown.

"The air fresheners!" exclaimed Willey. "So that's what Mum and Dad are up to!"

"Yes," replied Dudley "You are right – and now your mum and dad are becoming so transparent, there is a danger they may soon disappear completely, unless you are able to save them."

Dudley continued: "It appeared that Trickletown was doomed, until one night a small orange planet (Planet Fuddle) noticed something – one of the long-lost Fuddles was peering back at him! It was you, Willey, on the night before your birthday." *If you remember this was where our story began.* "And as you slept, a plan was put in place to bring you home again.

"Planet Fuddle was also in Trouble … The *nasty* Mr Got-a-Lott had arrived there with the Hour Glass Key, and with the help of the Mists of Time and the controlling powers of the Rainbow fish, they began to freeze Planet Fuddle's Water. They had hoped this would keep the Queen of Fuddles trapped there in her Golden Palace, and well away from their attempts to steal the Million Wiggle Fish and take over Trickletown. They know the Queen of Fuddles is the only one with the powers to stop them.

"But their plan has gone wrong! The Queen had come up with a cunning plan of her own, and together with the Orange Envelope, began to guide you, Willey, on your adventure and your quest, to find the Hour Glass Key and the Emerald Ring."

Mrs What'Nott, Mr What'Nott and Mr Got-a-Lott.
If you look very carefully you can almost see straight through them!

171

Willey was relieved, and nervous, as he was now fairly certain that his *friendly* mum and dad, his sister Casey and of course his pet dog Badsey, although they were being held by the Mists of Time, at least were somewhere safe. All he would need to do was succeed in his adventure. If he could find the Hour Glass Key and the Emerald Ring and bring them back to the centre of Trickletown with the Rainbow Fish, the magic at the centre of The Gambit would begin to work again, and his family could then return back home, down Rainbow Walk. As for his other mum and dad and Mr Got-a-Lott (the *nasty,* almost invisible ones), dealing with them might be a bit more difficult, as the Mists of Time were in control of them.

Willey needed more answers. "But how will we all return to Planet Fuddle?" he asked. *"And who was that grabbing hold of the Emerald Ring?"*

Willey paused and looked at Dudley, in the hope of one or two answers.

"Time has yet to tell us all its secrets," Dudley replied. "But I know the Emerald Ring will be close at hand when you need to use it. The feathers of the Rainbow Stork will take you back to Planet Fuddle. Follow the bubbles of the Million Wiggle Fish – they will take you where you need to go."

"The Million Wiggle Fish!" gasped Willey. "I, I, I am ..." Willey stuttered and paused. " ... I am afraid Good Old Henry might have eaten them!"

It appeared that Willey was right – the jar of Wiggle Fish was nowhere to be seen.

Fetch began sniffing at the air ... Eddy searched the area ... Brown Bottom pecked at the dust ... but the fish could not be found. Then Willey noticed the bubbles!

The Talking Teapot was giggling!

"There is no need to worry," chuckled Teabags, lifting his lid. "I tipped them all safely in here, before Good Old Henry grabbed hold of the jar."

There was a huge sigh of relief.

Willey needed more answers. "But what has happened to the Hour Glass Key and the Rainbow Fish?" he asked. "And who was that grabbing hold of the Emerald Ring?"

Willey paused and looked at Dudley, in the hope of one or two answers.

"Then there is no more time to waste," said Dudley. "Summon the Rainbow Stork!"

His command echoed around the caverns of the Sack of Secrets. It was not very long before they could hear the sound of flapping wings heading towards them.

Dudley gave out his final instructions: "'Port-Isaac' the Rainbow Stork will carry you out of the sack. She will give you five of her feathers – glide on them back to Planet Fuddle and into the Mists of Time. The Mists of Time are spreading throughout the Universe and have already tightened their grip around Planet Fuddle. Follow the Million Wiggle Fish bubbles – they will lead you to the seven Rainbow Fish. But you will need to be careful. There are dangers hidden in the Mists!

Seven icy glaciers hold the Moving Mountains prisoner and until the mountains are released, the water cannot flow to the King and Queen of Fuddles' Golden Palace. You must release the Hour Glass Key with the Emerald Ring to unfreeze the water.

"The King and Queen await you at the Golden Palace if you succeed.

"Above all, when you find it, *you must guard the Emerald Ring.* If the Mists of Time get hold of it, you may never see Trickletown again!"

"The Rainbow Stork will carry you out of the sack. She will give you five of her feathers — glide on them back to Planet Fuddle and into the Mists of Time."

- Chapter 17 -

The Moving Mountains

Old Man Moon and his Sack of Secrets were now far behind them and 'Port-Isaac' the Rainbow Stork had left them too. They were gliding on five of her feathers and below them were the Mists of Time; Willey and his friends would soon be landing back on Planet Fuddle.

Willey, Eddy, Teabags, Fetch and Brown Bottom drifted silently down, not daring to make a sound. They remembered Dudley's words and final instructions: "Follow the Million Wiggle Fish bubbles – they will lead you to the Rainbow Fish. But you will need to be careful, as there are dangers hidden in the Mist."

Willey was about to face the biggest challenge of his adventure.

'Touch down,' thought Willey, as his feather finally landed.

He was standing on the top of a mountain covered in ice. Willey had never been so frightened; everything was cold and still. He zipped up his jacket to the top and looked for the others. But all he could see was mist.

Beside him towered an Orange Rainbow Fish, staring back at him from its frozen prison of ice.

Willey remembered how the Rainbow Fish hovered around the Million Wiggle Fish Pond at the centre of Trickletown. They guarded the sluice which controlled the flow of the water running beneath it. And now the Mists of Time were using the powers of the Rainbow Fish to freeze the water on Planet Fuddle.

They were gliding on five of her feathers and below them were the Mists of Time;
Willey and his friends would soon be landing back on Planet Fuddle.

"EDDY!" shouted Willey. "TEABAGS! FETCH! BROWN BOTTOM!"

Surely his friends must have landed? But there was no reply. He felt nervous. The ground in front of him shuddered and started to move. Then, just like the Million Wiggle Fish Pond used to appear from beneath the ground at the centre of Trickletown, a magnificent crystal fountain rose up from the ice and settled itself in front of him.

"Welcome," said a voice from inside the fountain. A face was beginning to appear. As the icy form changed shape, Willey could see who it was. It was the missing Mr Got-a-Lott! He was the one who had stolen the Hour Glass Key and the Rainbow Fish from Trickletown. His face had almost turned to ice and he was wearing an icicle-shaped false moustache!

"Welcome," said Mr Got-a-Lott. "Welcome to the beginning of an icy end!" He laughed menacingly; then his face turned red with anger. "GIVE ME THE EMERALD RING OR YOU WILL NEVER SEE TRICKLETOWN AGAIN!" His bellowing voice forced back the swirling mist – and there were the Talking Teapot, Brown Bottom, Fetch and Eddy, frozen in blocks of ice!

Willey could see all the Rainbow Fish too, and an icy Key Stone, and there was the Hour Glass Key. *The one he had come for.*

'The Emerald Ring,' thought Willey. 'Where is it?'

What had Dudley said? 'I know the ring will be close when you need to use it.'

So where was the Emerald Ring?

Then, just like the Million Wiggle Fish Pond used to appear from beneath the ground at the centre of Trickletown, a magnificent crystal fountain rose up from the ice and settled itself in front of him.

Mr Got-a-Lott's face became redder and hotter. The hotter his face became, the more the ice rocks melted. He needed the Emerald Ring to lock the Hour Glass Key in its place. Then there would be nothing the Queen of Fuddles could do to stop him. Planet Fuddle's water would be frozen for ever and the secrets of Trickletown Valleys' Crater would belong to him and the Mists of Time.

Willey needed to think quickly …

The powers of the Rainbow Fish had frozen the water, but now the fish were prisoners themselves. If only he could find the Emerald Ring, he could place it in the frozen Key Stone and all of their troubles might be over.

Then suddenly a voice called out: "CATCH!" It was Teabags, Mr Got-a-Lott's red-hot face had melted his ice block.

The Talking Teapot's lid came spinning through the air towards Willey. "The ring is on top of my lid. Release the Hour Glass Key and let's get out of here!"

Sure enough, there was the missing Emerald Ring. It had been with them all the time and nobody knew it.

Everything now made perfect sense. This was why the Orange Envelope had told Willey to find the Talking Teapot, before he went on his journey to find the Hour Glass Key. It was the Talking Teapot's mysterious hand that had grabbed the Emerald Ring, when the Trouble in Trickletown began.

Willey caught the Teapot's lid and raced to the Key Stone.

"STOP HIM! STOP THAT BOY!" roared Mr Got-a-Lott – and before Willey could reach the Key Stone there was danger all around him!

"CATCH!" shouted Teabags. The Talking Teapot's lid came spinning through the air towards Willey.

Seven Crystal Cats now stood guard over the Rainbow Fish. An ugly creature ran out of the melting ice – it was a Mountain Groll. It was small and greenish-blue, with large hairy feet, but its muscles were strong. It threw itself at Willey and stole the Ring from his fingers.

"BRING ME THE EMERALD RING!" ordered Mr Got-a-Lott; but before the Groll could reach him, Fetch wriggled free from the melting ice and grabbed its arm.

Everything was happening at once! Willey's friends had now all broken free from the ice, but Fetch was in trouble – a crystal cat had cornered him.

The Talking Teapot tried to confuse their opponents; Eddy fought with the Cats; and Brown Bottom flew at the Groll.

The Emerald Ring dropped to the ground. This was Willey's chance, so he grabbed it and ran to the Key Stone. Nothing could stop him now! The moment the Ring found its place in the Hour Glass Key, the fighting stopped.

Mr Got-a-Lott's frozen face disappeared as the Ice Fountain melted. In its place stood the *real* Mr Got-a-Lott, now free from the ice and the Mists of Time.

"Quick," said Mr Got-a-Lott, jumping aboard the Red Rainbow Fish, "Follow me, and without any questions, they did. Everyone jumped aboard a Rainbow Fish and followed Mr Got-a-Lott down the mountain.

The Crystal Cats tried to follow. They pounced, but dissolved in the melting ice.

All of the adventurers were free; Willey had the Hour Glass Key and the Emerald Ring, and now they were heading down a melting glacier in the direction of the King and Queen of Fuddles' Golden Palace.

This was Willey's chance, so he grabbed it and ran to the Key Stone. Nothing could stop him now! The moment the Ring found its place in the Hour Glass Key, the fighting stopped.

"Yippee," shouted Teabags, as his Violet Rainbow Fish sped forward to the front.

Not to be outdone by a Talking Teapot, Mr Got-a-Lott inched his way back to regain the lead.

"Cock-a-Doodly-Doo!" cried Brown Bottom and Fetch together, giggling as they surfed between the two of them.

It had now become a race to the bottom of the Moving Mountains.

Willey smiled. His journey was almost at an end. He began to think of home and a safe return to Trickletown ...

"PRUSSIAN URSUS ARCTOS HORRIBLIS" shouted Mr Got-a-Lott, his face etched with fear. "LOOK OUT FOR THE BLUE GRIZZLY BEARS!"

The dangers of their visit to the mountains were certainly not over. The Blue Mountain Bears looked hungry and their favourite dinner was *fish*.

The Bears' sharp paws, teeth and claws thrashed at the water. The Rainbow Fish darted between whirlpools and swam with great speed around the rocks. They even blew colourful bubbles to churn up the water – until finally they made their escape and the danger was over.

"Cock-a-Doodly-Doo!"
cried Brown Bottom and Fetch together, giggling as they surfed.
It had now become a race to the bottom of the Moving Mountains.

None of the fish were caught; everyone had reached the Golden Palace.

The edge of the bank was lined with cheering Fuddles.

"Hurray for Willey What'Nott!"

"Three cheers for the Knick-Knack Tree Adventurers!"

"Hip Hip Hurray."

The King presented Willey with a Knick-Knack. This was Fuddle tradition at the end of an adventure.

"Hang this gold medallion on the Knick-Knack Tree's branches," said the King. "It will remind you of your adventure."

Willey promised he would; but his adventure was not quite over.

There was still a Chaseboard Challenge to be won, and who was going to win the Trickletown Valleys' Games' Grand Trophy?

Willey looked back over his shoulder – there was the Rainbow of Light, leading back to the Golden Ring of his Time-Line. It was time he was heading back to Trickletown Valleys' Crater.

Willey said good bye to his friends and ran towards the end of his Rainbow. "See you all in Trickletown!" Willey shouted – and then he was gone.

The King presented Willey with a Knick-Knack. "Hang this golden Knick-Knack on the Knick-Knack Tree's branches" said the King. "It will remind you of your adventure."

- Chapter 18 -

Return to Trickletown

The Rainbow of Light took Willey safely back to Trickletown. It left him standing on his Chaseboard, exactly in the position he had left it – near to the entrance of Blue Street Mine – and there was the Golden Ring of his Time-Line, balancing on the tip of his Chaseboard.

Everything was still frozen in time.

Willey moved himself back into racing position and looked around. There was no one else to be seen, so he placed the Golden Ring of his Time-Line back on his finger.

W O O O S H! Willey's Chaseboard sprang into action. It took him straight through a gap between some bushes and followed the course of a stream to open ground. The mist was still fairly thick, but the entrance to Blue Street Mine was just about visible.

'Where were all the others?' thought Willey. Surely the Chaseboard Challenge could not have finished without him?

Willey checked the colour of his tip-light: it was still shining green. This meant he was leading the Challenge, but he wasn't certain. He looked at his race-time indicator: the Challenge was almost over. Only ten more seconds remained. Willey counted them down one by one, whilst keeping a watchful eye out for his opponents: TEN ... NINE ... EIGHT ... SEVEN ... SIX ... FIVE ... FOUR ... THREE ... TWO ... ONE ... Then his Chaseboard played its victory chime – *Willey had won the Chaseboard Challenge for Orange Street!*

The crowds down in Trickletown erupted! Willey could hear the distant sound of voices and they were shouting and cheering his name.

Then, one by one, the rest of the Chaseboard Challengers began to appear from the entrance to Blue Street Mine. Ruby Taught'It from

Red Street arrived in second position; Trigger Moss from Green Street came third. They were followed by Tzahov Lemon; Eve Austin; then Baz (Basil Bun from Blue Street). But where was Zack Cubonyento? All he had needed to do was to finish the Challenge and Indigo Street would have won the Trickletown Valleys' Games' Grand Trophy.

Everyone looked at the scoreboard. The Indigo Street Fuddles were worried! They had always won the Grand Trophy, but this year Orange Street was close.

Then the scoreboard flashed the result: *Zack Cubonyento Zero Points – DNF (Did Not Finish).* Orange Street had won – HURRAY! The celebrations began with fireworks – and most of the fireworks were *orange!*

Although Willey was excited and could not wait to get back to Trickletown and join in with the celebrations, he was worried about Zack. They had never really been the best of friends, but they were after all both Fuddles – and Fuddles in times of trouble look after each other. "Once a Fuddle always a Fuddle," you would hear them say about each other. So Willey headed back to the other side of the Crater and down into the murky tunnels of Orange Street Mine. He fumbled around in his pocket for the map that Teabags had given him:

'*Turn right, to avoid the entrance to Trickletown's Labyrinths.*

Left and immediately down, before the Sticky Rocks grab you.

Take your chance through the Cavern of Tricks.

Right, left and right around the Cauldron of Indigo Basin and then up until you reach the all-seeing eye of Blue Street Labyrinth.'

It did not take very long before Willey found him. Zack was dangling by the seat of his pants, stuck to a large sticky rock on the roof of Orange Street Mine.

Willey could not stop giggling!

"Stay exactly where you are," chuckled Willey, doing his best not to laugh too loudly.

"I'll go and get help. So don't wriggle about too much in those trousers or you might fall out of them."

Zack immediately stopped wriggling; but help had already arrived. The Cubonyento Brothers had followed Willey into the mine and it was only a matter of moments before Zack was free, but his trousers remained stuck to a large sticky rock! Willey chuckled again.

Everyone returned to Trickletown. The Grand Trophy was presented to Orange Street, and Willey was the hero of the Games. But amongst all the celebrations and laughter something sinister was happening. No one had noticed that the Mists were rolling in!

Willey had forgotten all about the Hour Glass Key. It was tucked inside his jacket, and in the excitement he had forgotten about his friends on Planet Fuddle, who were waiting to return.

The 'memory-loss' spray was still working – and even though some of the Fuddles had begun to wonder why Mr and Mrs What'Nott and Mr Got-a-Lott were now almost invisible, the Mists of Time were finally taking over Trickletown.

Mr and Mrs What'Nott were laughing, but they hadn't realised that they themselves had been tricked by the Mists – their bodies were beginning to disappear and now they were so transparent, there was a danger they might vanish completely.

Even after Willey's long adventure it appeared that the Mists of Time were going to win.

*It did not take very long before Willey found him. Zack was dangling by the seat
of his pants, stuck to a large sticky rock on the roof of Orange Street Mine.
Willey could not stop giggling!*

Then suddenly the Mayor of Trickletown noticed something. Something bright, which was shining on Willey's hand! "THE EMERALD GREEN RELEASE RING!" shouted the Mayor. The glow of the Emerald Ring had jogged his memory – and just in time.

Willey looked at the Emerald Ring, and then at the thickening mist. "The Hour Glass Key!" gasped Willey. He grabbed it from inside his jacket and ran to the Key Stone.

The anxious figures of Mr and Mrs What'Nott raced to stop him, but Willey was far too quick. He placed the Hour Glass Key in the Key Stone and then 'unlocked' it with the Emerald Ring.

A bright green glow flashed across the hamlets of Trickletown and thunder rumbled in the mountains. The Mists of Time rolled back to the edge of the Crater; they could stay no longer. Mr and Mrs What'Notts' disappearing bodies slowly returned and all of the Fuddles' memories came flooding back again.

Trickletown was saved!

Willey looked at the Emerald Ring, and then at the thickening mist. "The Hour Glass Key!" gasped Willey. He grabbed it from inside his jacket and ran to the Key Stone.

The ground at the centre of The Gambit started to move. Everyone stood perfectly still and watched, as the magic at the centre of Trickletown unfolded in front of them.

The circle of oak trees quivered and stretched out their branches. Then, from the inner end of Lock Street, a colourful, spiral pathway appeared. This was Rainbow Walk – a passageway in and out of time – 'A place where adventures begin and dreams come true'. As the spiral pathway reached the centre of The Gambit, a living granite rock rose up from the ground. It hovered high above the oak trees and gradually changed its shape into a silver fish, its scales all shimmering with gold. The eyes of the fish scanned Trickletown. It was looking for any sign of danger, but the Mists of Time were gone, banished beyond the mountains. When the fish was sure that everything around it was safe, a magical and glorious fish pond appeared from beneath the ground. Its crystal clear waters teamed with colourful fish – the Million Wiggle Fish Pond had returned! Everyone cheered.

"LOOK!" shouted Willey, pointing among the hazy colours of Rainbow Walk. "Here come the Rainbow Fish!"

He was right – the Seven Rainbow Fish had returned to Trickletown and taking up their positions around the fish pond, they released a flow of water over The Gambit. Seven streams flowed out into Trickletown's rivers and soon the mystical powers of the Million Wiggle Fish Pond were able to work again.

"LOOK!" shouted Willey, pointing among the hazy colours of Rainbow Walk
"Here come the RainbowFish!"
He was right – the Seven Rainbow Fish had returned to Trickletown.

"EDDY!" shouted Willey. "TEABAGS!"

"FETCH!" yelled Farmer Crisp, from his wheelchair.

"COCK-A-DOODLY-DOO!" replied Brown Bottom.

"MR GOT-A-LOTT!" shouted the Mayor.

Everyone laughed and cheered as the intrepid band of adventurers returned to Trickletown.

Everyone laughed and cheered as the intrepid band of adventurers returned to Trickletown.

"BADSEY! IT'S BADSEY!" shouted Willey excitedly, as a small dog charged down Rainbow Walk to greet him. Badsey was followed by Willey's missing mum and dad and his sister, Casey. Willey ran into his family's arms and they hugged and kissed him. They no longer had divided bodies – everyone in the What'Nott family was back together again, just as they had been before Willey's adventures began.

Willey ran into his family's arms and they hugged and kissed him.

So, was this finally the end of Willey's Adventure? Well, yes it was – almost!

A small brown owl had glided silently down Rainbow Walk. "Ta'wit-ta'whoo," said the owl, as she headed over The Gambit and up the Emerald Causeway.

She was heading for the Emerald Forest, in the direction of a very important tree. Gone was Cedric's Field and gone was the Bank of Thorns – the Knick-Knack Tree was safe. As the owl arrived, the Knick-Knack Tree just smiled and bowed its branches – you see this was no ordinary owl! The owl had been controlling Willey's adventure from the very start; from the moment he looked out of his bedroom window, on the night before his birthday and saw the eyes of Planet Fuddle staring back at him. The owl was not only the messenger, she was the Queen of Fuddles herself – a sorceress whose power equalled that of the Mists of Time.

*

Knicky-Knacky leaned back on his favourite log and looked around. There were many Fuddle-like faces staring back at him. His story about the 'Trouble in Trickletown' had come to an end, but the Knick-Knack Tree's magic was still surrounding them.

As the owl arrived, the Knick-Knack Tree just smiled and bowed its branches – for this was no ordinary owl! The owl was not only a messenger, she was the Queen of Fuddles herself.

It was time to hang the Gold Medallion back on the Knick-Knack Tree's branches.

The glow bees buzzed with excitement as Knicky-Knacky climbed to the top. When the Knick-Knack was returned to its rightful place, the Knick-Knack Tree smiled. The magic of the adventure then faded away and everyone cheered!

What became of the other Mr Got-a-Lott – the one with the *curly* false moustache? He never returned to Trickletown. He stayed aboard the Pie-Rats' Galleon in search of a new adventure. Cedric was never seen again; and Pickle, the magic Rainbow-hopper, continued to have fun around Trickletown with Colonel Tuft and his Under-Cover Grass Army, playing tricks on each other whenever they could get away with it.

And Willey's Special Birthday Surprise – apart from the mysterious circus ticket? Well, this was a solar-powered scooter. His mum and dad had hidden it under a pile of sacks in Willey's bike shed.

As for the Fuddles now living in Trickletown Valleys' Crater, they all went home again, and for the moment, or at least until the next Knick-Knack Tree Adventure, everyone was very good friends with everyone else.

"Cock-a-Doodly-Doo!" crowed Brown Bottom.

Indigo Basin went 'BOOM!'

It must be 5 o'clock.

It was time to hang the Gold Medallion back on the Knick-Knack Tree's branches. The glow bees buzzed with excitement as Knicky-Knacky climbed to the top.

A Message about *'Secrets'* from Dudley

S ecrets can exist for many different reasons. Some are secrets to be kept and others are secrets to be broken.

'Secrets to be kept' are real secrets – like the secret password to your computer and sometimes even where you live. These are things you should never tell a stranger.

'Secrets to be broken' are written by children who are sad and being teased or bullied at school. These are secrets you should really be telling a grown-up. So if you are being bullied at school, why not write a letter to Dudley or draw him a picture? Then you could give it to your mum or dad, or a teacher.

Dudley reads all of the secrets he receives, and he never tells them to anyone who shouldn't know about them. He always does his best to make everyone feel happy in the end.

There are of course many **'Secrets made for fun'**. So enjoy making lots of different secrets. Dudley always loves to eat the funny ones.

Dudley – the Keeper of Secrets has arrived on Planet Earth.
There will be no more bullying in schools.

Knick-Knack Tree Adventures

Photograph by A E Buckley

Could you be the author of our next Knick-Knack Tree Adventure?

Wiggly-Fish Books offers opportunities for talented short story, novel and script writers for our Knick-Knack Tree Adventure character groups. Visit our website for up-to-date information.

www.wiggly-fish.com

Martin Buckley
A Message from the Author

The idea of the Knick-Knack Tree Adventures began a decade before a novel had even been thought about. A bedtime story was needed one night, in a holiday cottage in Port Isaac, Cornwall, England – and with no books around there was only one thing to do: make one up.

The 'Knick-Knack Tree Adventures' were born, and there was no turning back. Ideas were created, characters emerged, models were made and my imagination went into overdrive.

However, every attempt to succeed was met by apparent failure. "What is it all about?" everyone asked. Try answering a question like that in 30 seconds before your audience begins to get bored! So I decided to write down the story so that everyone could read all about it.

In December 2010, in front of a fire in a draughty living room, in the Worcestershire village of Badsey, the story began. The many ideas in my head began forming themselves on my laptop. However, I very soon realised I had no real story at all. Just cameos of excitement: a Million Wiggle Fish Pond; a cockerel called Brown Bottom; a circus; Old Man Moon; an adventurer called Willey What'Nott; The Pie-Rat Gang; Knicky-Knacky and the Knick-Knack Tree; and numerous other characters and places.

The story evolved by creating pictures in my mind; and then moving the characters through them. There were many problems to solve. Where could the adventure take place? Who were these characters and how had they got there? I kept a note pad next to my bed, went for walks up Bredon Hill, and bounced ideas off anyone who would listen. After moving to Beckford, I asked friends and family for advice and support. The task seemed endless; in fact, it took almost 2 years and then I decided to illustrate it. Eventually the story was finally complete. The first Knick-Knack Tree Adventure had arrived: *Trouble in Trickletown*.

ACKNOWLEDGEMENTS

This Knick-Knack Tree Adventure would never have been completed without
the help and support of friends, family and the many readers, both children
and adults, who gave their views along the way.

Special thanks to:

Carolyn Middleton, proof reading and story continuity

Angela Devereux, first proof copy editing and proof reading

Andrea Rayner, finished story copy editing and proof reading

John Green, information technology

Dorothy M. Mitchell, author of period novels, children's stories and poems,
for her inspiration, support and friendship

Phil Harding of the Time Team series (Channel 4)
for his endorsement of the character Phil Dug'It,
for which he was the inspiration

Paul and Doreen Buckley (Mum & Dad) for dinners, cups of tea and coffee,
wake-up calls, a roof over my head whilst writing and illustrating this story …
and much more …

THANK YOU ALL

Knick-Knack Tree Adventures

Supporters of Anti-Bullying

Dudley - the Keeper of Secrets.
There will be no more Bullying in Schools.

See Dudley's Message about Secrets and Bullying on page 202
or visit our website: www.wiggly-fish.com